The Prospect of Flowers

Ruskin Bond has been writing for over sixty years, and now has over 120 titles in print—novels, collections of short stories, poetry, essays, anthologies and books for children. His first novel, *The Room on the Roof*, received the prestigious John Llewellyn Rhys Award in 1957. He has also received the Padma Shri (1999), the Padma Bhushan (2014) and two awards from Sahitya Akademi—one for his short stories and another for his writings for children. In 2012, the Delhi government gave him its Lifetime Achievement Award.

Born in 1934, Ruskin Bond grew up in Jamnagar, Shimla, New Delhi and Dehradun. Apart from three years in the UK, he has spent all his life in India, and now lives in Mussoorie with his adopted family.

RUSKIN BOND

The Prospect of Flowers

RUPA

Published by
Rupa Publications India Pvt. Ltd 2016
7/16, Ansari Road, Daryaganj
New Delhi 110002

Sales centres:
Prayagraj Bengaluru Chennai
Hyderabad Jaipur Kathmandu
Kolkata Mumbai

P-ISBN: 978-81-291-4210-8
E-ISBN: 978-81-291-4632-8

Fifth impression 2023

10 9 8 7 6 5

Printed in India

Contents

Introduction

Walking around Himalayan towns, villages and forests, I have found many of my characters as they have strolled by, stopping to spend the time of day with me. Ambling down a hilly road, carrying an umbrella to keep away the pattering rain, stopping to admire the flowers growing wild on the mountainside—these are things I do every day, and what life in the mountains is often about.

I don't think some of these stories or characters could have lived and grown anywhere else. Could Binya with her blue umbrella have lived anywhere but in a mountain village with its tiny population of eccentric characters? Hilltops and mountainsides are the perfect setting for otherworldly people and happenings, including long dead masters appearing after years as in 'Gone Fishing' or the surreal 'On Fairy Hill'. Adventure and intrigue lurk in rocky cliffs and shadowy recesses. Imagine grazing your sheep in the high mountains and then having to fight off an eagle determined to make off with one of the flock as Jai did in 'The Eyes of the Eagle'.

Connections that form between men, women and children disregarding the divisions of age and across the stages of life is something that fascinates me. A substantial part of my own childhood was spent in the company of my grandparents and this had a lasting impact. Among these stories, 'The Cherry Tree' is perhaps the most special. From a seed that Rakesh saves while eating cherries, grows a plant that becomes a tree despite setbacks of weather and the careless swish of a sickle. As Rakesh grows, so does the tree, and both are guided into their lives by Grandfather.

It is among these mountains that I have also found lifelong friends and companions. 'From Small Beginnings' is about how Prem came into my life. One day a young man appeared, looking for work, like so many hill people who have to move away from their villages. From that time, Prem kept drifting in and out of my life for many years, sometimes in the employ of the government, and others in the home of the school headmaster. When Prem and the headmaster's wife finally fell out, he came to me and became the first member of my ever-expanding family.

It's perhaps impossible to fathom how much the mountains have permeated my life and writing. I lived in the plains in my youth in order to make a living, but when the opportunity came, I went back to where my heart lay. My fifty years in Mussoorie are an epic in themselves. I do go away sometimes but I always return in some haste to my small study with its window looking out upon the mountains and the valley. Every writer needs a window. Preferably two.

The inspiration I draw while sitting at my windows is mirrored in the pages of this book. The people who pass through, the little insects that buzz in and out, the birds that call out to me, the mountain and trees that stand there, eternal yet forever changing—these are the worlds I wish to preserve for my readers.

Ruskin Bond

The Prospect of Flowers

FERN HILL, THE OAKS, HUNTER'S LODGE, THE PARSONAGE, THE Pines, Dumbarnie, Mackinnon's Hall and Windermere. These are the names of some of the old houses that still stand on the outskirts of one of the smaller Indian hill stations. Most of them have fallen into decay and ruin. They are very old, of course—built over a hundred years ago by Britishers who sought relief from the searing heat of the plains. Today's visitors to the hill stations prefer to live near the markets and cinemas, and many of the old houses, set amidst oak and maple and deodar, are inhabited by wildcats, bandicoots, owls, goats and the occasional charcoal burner or mule driver.

But amongst these neglected mansions stands a neat, whitewashed cottage called Mulberry Lodge. And in it, up to a short time ago, lived an elderly English spinster named Miss Mackenzie.

In years Miss Mackenzie was more than 'elderly', being well over eighty. But no one would have guessed it. She was clean, sprightly, and wore old-fashioned but well-preserved dresses. Once a week, she walked the two miles to town to buy butter and jam and soap and sometimes a small bottle of eau de cologne.

She had lived in the hill station since she had been a girl in her teens, and that had been before the First World War. Though she had never married, she had experienced a few love affairs and was far from being the typical frustrated spinster of fiction. Her parents had been dead thirty years; her brother and sister were also dead. She had no relatives in India, and she lived on a small pension of forty rupees a month and the gift parcels that were sent out to her from New Zealand by a friend of her youth.

Like other lonely old people, she kept a pet—a large black cat with bright yellow eyes. In her small garden she grew dahlias, chrysanthemums, gladioli and a few rare orchids. She knew a great deal about plants and about wild flowers, trees, birds and insects. She had never made a serious study of these things, but having lived with them for so many years had developed an intimacy with all that grew and flourished around her.

She had few visitors. Occasionally, the padre from the local church called on her, and once a month the postman came with a letter from New Zealand or her pension papers. The milkman called every second day with a litre of milk for the lady and her cat. And sometimes she received a couple of eggs free, for the egg seller remembered a time when Miss Mackenzie, in her earlier prosperity, had bought eggs from him in large quantities. He was a sentimental man. He remembered her as a ravishing beauty in her twenties when he had gazed at her in round-eyed, nine-year-old wonder and consternation.

Now it was September and the rains were nearly over, and Miss Mackenzie's chrysanthemums were coming into their own. She hoped the coming winter wouldn't be too severe because she found it increasingly difficult to bear the cold.

One day, as she was pottering about in her garden, she saw a schoolboy plucking wild flowers on the slope about the cottage.

'Who's that?' she called. 'What are you up to, young man?'

The boy was alarmed and tried to dash up the hillside, but he slipped on pine needles and came slithering down the slope on to Miss Mackenzie's nasturtium bed.

When he found there was no escape, he gave a bright disarming smile and said, 'Good morning, miss.'

He belonged to the local English-medium school and wore a bright red blazer and a red-and-black striped tie. Like most polite Indian schoolboys, he called every woman 'miss'.

'Good morning,' said Miss Mackenzie severely. 'Would you mind moving out of my flower bed?'

The boy stepped gingerly over the nasturtiums and looked up at Miss Mackenzie with dimpled cheeks and appealing eyes. It was impossible to be angry with him.

'You're trespassing,' said Miss Mackenzie.

'Yes, miss.'

'And you ought to be in school at this hour.'

'Yes, miss.'

'Then what are you doing here?'

'Picking flowers, miss.' And he held up a bunch of ferns and wild flowers.

'Oh.' Miss Mackenzie was disarmed. It was a long time since she had seen a boy taking an interest in flowers, and, what was more, playing truant from school in order to gather them.

'Do you like flowers?' she asked.

'Yes, miss. I'm going to be a botan—a botantist?'

'You mean a botanist.'

'Yes, miss.'

'Well, that's unusual. Most boys at your age want to be

pilots or soldiers or perhaps engineers. But you want to be a botanist. Well, well. There's still hope for the world, I see. And do you know the names of these flowers?'

'This is a *bukhilo* flower,' he said, showing her a small golden flower. 'That's a Pahari name. It means puja or prayer. The flower is offered during prayers. But I don't know what this is…'

He held out a pale pink flower with a soft, heart-shaped leaf.

'It's a wild begonia,' said Miss Mackenzie. 'And that purple stuff is salvia, but it isn't wild. It's a plant that escaped from my garden. Don't you have any books on flowers?'

'No, miss.'

'All right, come in and I'll show you a book.'

She led the boy into a small front room, which was crowded with furniture and books and vases and jam jars, and offered him a chair. He sat awkwardly on its edge. The black cat immediately leapt on to his knees, and settled down on them, purring loudly.

'What's your name?' asked Miss Mackenzie, as she rummaged through her books.

'Anil, miss.'

'And where do you live?'

'When school closes, I go to Delhi. My father has a business.'

'Oh, and what's that?'

'Bulbs, miss.'

'Flower bulbs?'

'No, electric bulbs.'

'Electric bulbs! You might send me a few, when you get home. Mine are always fusing, and they're so expensive, like everything else these days. Ah, here we are!' She pulled a heavy volume down from the shelf and laid it on the table. '*Flora Himaliensis,* published in 1892, and probably the only copy in India. This is a very valuable book, Anil. No other naturalist has recorded so many wild Himalayan flowers. And let me tell you this, there are many flowers and plants which are still unknown to the fancy botanists who spend all their time with microscopes instead of in the mountains. But perhaps, *you'll* do something about that, one day.'

'Yes, miss.'

They went through the book together, and Miss Mackenzie pointed out many flowers that grew in and around the hill station, while the boy made notes of their names and seasons. She lit a stove, and put the kettle on for tea. And then the old English lady and the small Indian boy sat side by side over cups of hot sweet tea, absorbed in a book on wild flowers.

'May I come again?' asked Anil, when finally he rose to go.

'If you like,' said Miss Mackenzie. 'But not during school hours. You mustn't miss your classes.'

After that, Anil visited Miss Mackenzie about once a week, and nearly always brought a wild flower for her to identify. She found herself looking forward to the boy's visits—and sometimes, when more than a week passed and he didn't come, she was disappointed and lonely and would grumble at the black cat.

Anil reminded her of her brother, when the latter had been a boy. There was no physical resemblance. Andrew had been fair- haired and blue-eyed. But it was Anil's eagerness, his alert, bright look and the way he stood—legs apart, hands on hips, a picture of confidence—that reminded her of the boy who had shared her own youth in these same hills.

And why did Anil come to see her so often?

Partly because she knew about wild flowers, and he really did want to become a botanist. And partly because she smelt of freshly baked bread, and that was a smell his own grandmother had possessed. And partly because she was lonely and sometimes a boy of twelve can sense loneliness better than an adult. And partly because he was a little different from other children.

By the middle of October, when there was only a fortnight left for the school to close, the first snow had fallen on the distant mountains. One peak stood high above the rest, a white pinnacle against the azure-blue sky. When the sun set, this peak turned from orange to gold to pink to red.

'How high is that mountain?' asked Anil.

'It must be over twelve thousand feet,' said Miss Mackenzie. 'About thirty miles from here, as the crow flies. I always wanted to go there, but there was no proper road. At that height, there'll be flowers that you don't get here—the blue gentian and the purple columbine, the anemone and the edelweiss.'

'I'll go there one day,' said Anil.

'I'm sure you will, if you really want to.'

The day before his school closed, Anil came to say goodbye to Miss Mackenzie.

I don't suppose you'll be able to find many wild flowers in Delhi,' she said. 'But have a good holiday.'

"Thank you, miss.'

As he was about to leave, Miss Mackenzie, on an impulse, thrust the *Flora Himaliensis* into his hands.

'You keep it,' she said. 'It's a present for you.'

'But I'll be back next year, and I'll be able to look at it then. It's so valuable.'

'I know it's valuable and that's why I've given it to you. Otherwise it will only fall into the hands of the junk dealers.'

'But, miss...'

'Don't argue. Besides, I may not be here next year.'

'Are you going away?'

'I'm not sure. I may go to England.'

She had no intention of going to England; she had not seen the country since she was a child, and she knew she would not fit in with the life of post-war Britain. Her home was in these hills, among the oaks and maples and deodars. It was lonely, but at her age it would be lonely anywhere.

The boy tucked the book under his arm, straightened his tie, stood stiffly to attention and said, 'Goodbye, Miss Mackenzie.'

It was the first time he had spoken her name.

Winter set in early and strong winds brought rain and sleet, and soon there were no flowers in the garden or on the hillside. The cat stayed indoors, curled up at the foot of Miss Mackenzie's bed.

Miss Mackenzie wrapped herself up in all her old shawls and mufflers, but still she felt the cold. Her fingers grew so stiff that she took almost an hour to open a can of baked beans. And then it snowed and for several days the milkman did not come. The postman arrived with her pension papers, but she felt too tired to take them up to town to the bank.

She spent most of the time in bed. It was the warmest place. She kept a hot-water bottle at her back, and the cat kept her feet warm. She lay in bed, dreaming of the spring and summer months. In three months' time the primroses would be out, and with the coming of spring the boy would return.

One night the hot-water bottle burst and the bedding was soaked through. As there was no sun for several days, the blanket remained damp. Miss Mackenzie caught a chill and had to keep to her cold, uncomfortable bed. She knew she had a fever but there was no thermometer with which to take her temperature. She had difficulty in breathing.

A strong wind sprang up one night, and the window flew

open and kept banging all night. Miss Mackenzie was too weak to get up and close it, and the wind swept the rain and sleet into the room. The cat crept into the bed and snuggled close to its mistress's warm body. But towards morning that body had lost its warmth and the cat left the bed and started scratching about on the floor.

As a shaft of sunlight streamed through the open window, the milkman arrived. He poured some milk into the cat's saucer on the doorstep, and the cat leapt down from the windowsill and made for the milk.

The milkman called a greeting to Miss Mackenzie, but received no answer. Her window was open and he had always known her to be up before sunrise. So he put his head in at the window and called again. But Miss Mackenzie did not answer. She had gone away to the mountain where the blue gentian and purple columbine grew.

The Blue Umbrella

1

'NEELU! NEELU!' CRIED BINYA.

She scrambled barefoot over the rocks, ran over the short summer grass, up and over the brow of the hill, all the time calling 'Neelu, Neelu!'

Neelu—Blue—was the name of the blue-grey cow. The other cow, which was white, was called Gori, meaning Fair One. They were fond of wandering off on their own, down to the stream or into the pine forest, and sometimes they came back by themselves and sometimes they stayed away—almost deliberately, it seemed to Binya.

If the cows didn't come home at the right time, Binya would be sent to fetch them. Sometimes her brother, Bijju, went with her, but these days he was busy preparing for his exams and didn't have time to help with the cows.

Binya liked being on her own, and sometimes she allowed the cows to lead her into some distant valley, and then they would all be late coming home. The cows preferred having Binya with them, because she let them wander. Bijju pulled them by their tails if they went too far.

Binya belonged to the mountains, to this part of the Himalayas known as Garhwal. Dark forests and lonely hilltops held no terrors for her. It was only when she was in the market town, jostled by the crowds in the bazaar, that she felt rather nervous and lost. The town, five miles from the village, was also a pleasure resort for tourists from all over India.

Binya was probably ten. She may have been nine or even eleven, she couldn't be sure because no one in the village kept birthdays; but her mother told her she'd been born during a winter when the snow had come up to the windows, and that was just over ten years ago, wasn't it? Two years later, her father had died, but his passing had made no difference to their way of life. They had three tiny terraced fields on the side of the mountain, and they grew potatoes, onions, ginger, beans, mustard and maize: not enough to sell in the town, but enough to live on.

Like most mountain girls, Binya was quite sturdy, fair of skin, with pink cheeks and dark eyes and her black hair tied in a pigtail. She wore pretty glass bangles on her wrists, and a necklace of glass beads. From the necklace hung a leopard's claw. It was a lucky charm, and Binya always wore it. Bijju had one, too, only his was attached to a string.

Binya's full name was Binyadevi, and Bijju's real name was Vijay, but everyone called them Binya and Bijju. Binya was two years younger than her brother.

She had stopped calling for Neelu; she had heard the cowbells tinkling, and knew the cows hadn't gone far. Singing to herself, she walked over fallen pine needles into the forest glade on the spur of the hill. She heard voices, laughter, the clatter of plates and cups, and stepping through the trees, she came upon a party of picnickers.

They were holiday-makers from the plains. The women were dressed in bright saris, the men wore light summer shirts, and the children had pretty new clothes. Binya, standing in the shadows between the trees, went unnoticed; for some time she watched the picnickers, admiring their clothes, listening to their unfamiliar accents, and gazing rather hungrily at the sight of all their food. And then her gaze came to rest on a bright blue umbrella, a frilly thing for women, which lay open on the grass beside its owner.

Now Binya had seen umbrellas before, and her mother had a big black umbrella which nobody used any more because the field rats had eaten holes in it, but this was the first time Binya had seen such a small, dainty, colourful umbrella and she fell in love with it. The umbrella was like a flower, a great blue flower that had sprung up on the dry brown hillside.

She moved forward a few paces so that she could see the umbrella better. As she came out of the shadows into the sunlight, the picnickers saw her.

'Hello, look who's here!' exclaimed the older of the two women. 'A little village girl!'

'Isn't she pretty?' remarked the other. 'But how torn and dirty her clothes are!' It did not seem to bother them that Binya could hear and understand everything they said about her.

'They're very poor in the hills,' said one of the men.

'Then let's give her something to eat.' And the older woman beckoned to Binya to come closer.

Hesitantly, nervously, Binya approached the group. Normally she would have turned and fled, but the attraction was the pretty blue umbrella. It had cast a spell over her, drawing her forward almost against her will.

'What's that on her neck?' asked the younger woman.

'A necklace of sorts.'

'It's a pendant—see, there's a claw hanging from it!'

'It's a tiger's claw,' said the man beside her. (He had never seen a tiger's claw.) 'A lucky charm. These people wear them to keep away evil spirits.' He looked to Binya for confirmation, but Binya said nothing.

'Oh, I want one too!' said the woman, who was obviously his wife.

'You can't get them in shops.'

'Buy hers, then. Give her two or three rupees, she's sure to need the money.'

The man, looking slightly embarrassed but anxious to please his young wife, produced a two-rupee note and offered it to Binya, indicating that he wanted the pendant in exchange. Binya put her hand to the necklace, half afraid that the excited woman would snatch it away from her. Solemnly she shook her head. The man then showed her a five-rupee note, but again Binya shook her head.

'How silly she is!' exclaimed the young woman.

'It may not be hers to sell,' said the man. 'But I'll try again. How much do you want—what can we give you?' And he waved his hand towards the picnic things scattered about on the grass.

Without any hesitation Binya pointed to the umbrella.

'My umbrella!' exclaimed the young woman. 'She wants my umbrella. What cheek!'

'Well, you want her pendant, don't you?'

'That's different.'

'Is it?'

The man and his wife were beginning to quarrel with each other.

'I'll ask her to go away,' said the older woman. 'We're making such fools of ourselves.'

'But I want the pendant!' cried the other, petulantly. And then, on an impulse, she picked up the umbrella and held it out to Binya. 'Here, take the umbrella!'

Binya removed her necklace and held it out to the young woman, who immediately placed it around her own neck. Then Binya took the umbrella and held it up. It did not look so small in her hands; in fact, it was just the right size.

She had forgotten about the picnickers, who were busy examining the pendant. She turned the blue umbrella this way and that, looked through the bright blue silk at the pulsating sun, and then, still keeping it open, turned and disappeared into the forest glade.

2

Binya seldom closed the blue umbrella. Even when she had it in the house, she left it lying open in a corner of the room. Sometimes Bijju snapped it shut, complaining that it got in the way. She would open it again a little later. It wasn't beautiful when it was closed.

Whenever Binya went out—whether it was to graze the cows, or fetch water from the spring, or carry milk to the little tea shop on the Tehri road—she took the umbrella with her. That patch of sky-blue silk could always be seen on the hillside.

Old Ram Bharosa (Ram the Trustworthy) kept the tea shop on the Tehri road. It was a dusty, unmetalled road. Once a day, the Tehri bus stopped near his shop and passengers got down to sip hot tea or drink a glass of curd. He kept a few bottles of Coca-Cola too, but as there was no ice, the bottles got hot in the sun and so were seldom opened. He also kept sweets and toffees, and when Binya or Bijju had a few coins to spare, they would spend them at the shop. It was only a mile from the village.

Ram Bharosa was astonished to see Binya's blue umbrella.

'What have you there, Binya?' he asked.

Binya gave the umbrella a twirl and smiled at Ram Bharosa. She was always ready with her smile, and would willingly have lent it to anyone who was feeling unhappy.

'That's a lady's umbrella,' said Ram Bharosa. 'That's only for memsahibs. Where did you get it?'

'Someone gave it to me—for my necklace.'

'You exchanged it for your lucky claw!'

Binya nodded.

'But what do you need it for? The sun isn't hot enough, and it isn't meant for the rain. It's just a pretty thing for rich ladies to play with!'

Binya nodded and smiled again. Ram Bharosa was quite right; it was just a beautiful plaything. And that was exactly why she had fallen in love with it.

'I have an idea,' said the shopkeeper. 'It's no use to you, that umbrella. Why not sell it to me? I'll give you five rupees for it.'

'It's worth fifteen,' said Binya.

'Well, then, I'll give you ten.'

Binya laughed and shook her head.

'Twelve rupees?' said Ram Bharosa, but without much hope.

Binya placed a five-paise coin on the counter. 'I came for a toffee,' she said.

Ram Bharosa pulled at his drooping whiskers, gave Binya a wry look, and placed a toffee in the palm of her hand. He watched Binya as she walked away along the dusty road. The blue umbrella held him fascinated, and he stared after it until it was out of sight.

The villagers used this road to go to the market town. Some used the bus, a few rode on mules and most people walked. Today, everyone on the road turned their heads to stare at the girl with the bright blue umbrella.

Binya sat down in the shade of a pine tree. The umbrella, still open, lay beside her. She cradled her head in her arms, and presently she dozed off. It was that kind of day, sleepily warm and summery.

And while she slept, a wind sprang up.

It came quietly, swishing gently through the trees, humming softly. Then it was joined by other random gusts, bustling over the tops of the mountains. The trees shook their heads and came to life. The wind fanned Binya's cheeks. The umbrella stirred on the grass.

The wind grew stronger, picking up dead leaves and sending them spinning and swirling through the air. It got into the umbrella and began to drag it over the grass. Suddenly it lifted the umbrella and carried it about six feet from the sleeping girl. The sound woke Binya.

She was on her feet immediately, and then she was leaping down the steep slope. But just as she was within reach of the umbrella, the wind picked it up again and carried it further downhill.

Binya set off in pursuit. The wind was in a wicked, playful mood. It would leave the umbrella alone for a few moments but as soon as Binya came near, it would pick up the umbrella again and send it bouncing, floating, dancing away from her.

The hill grew steeper. Binya knew that after twenty yards

it would fall away in a precipice. She ran faster. And the wind ran with her, ahead of her, and the blue umbrella stayed up with the wind.

A fresh gust picked it up and carried it to the very edge of the cliff. There it balanced for a few seconds, before toppling over, out of sight.

Binya ran to the edge of the cliff. Going down on her hands and knees, she peered down the cliff face. About a hundred feet below, a small stream rushed between great boulders. Hardly anything grew on the cliff face—just a few stunted bushes, and, halfway down, a wild cherry tree growing crookedly out of the rocks and hanging across the chasm. The umbrella had stuck in the cherry tree.

Binya didn't hesitate. She may have been timid with strangers, but she was at home on a hillside. She stuck her bare leg over the edge of the cliff and began climbing down. She kept her face to the hillside, feeling her way with her feet, only changing her handhold when she knew her feet were secure. Sometimes she held on to the thorny bilberry bushes, but she did not trust the other plants which came away very easily.

Loose stones rattled down the cliff. Once on their way, the stones did not stop until they reached the bottom of the hill; and they took other stones with them, so that there was soon a cascade of stones, and Binya had to be very careful not to start a landslide.

As agile as a mountain goat, she did not take more than five minutes to reach the crooked cherry tree. But the most difficult task remained—she had to crawl along the trunk of the tree, which stood out at right angles from the cliff. Only by doing this could she reach the trapped umbrella.

Binya felt no fear when climbing trees. She was proud of

the fact that she could climb them as well as Bijju. Gripping the rough cherry bark with her toes, and using her knees as leverage, she crawled along the trunk of the projecting tree until she was almost within reach of the umbrella. She noticed with dismay that the blue cloth was torn in a couple of places.

She looked down, and it was only then that she felt afraid. She was right over the chasm, balanced precariously about eighty feet above the boulder-strewn stream. Looking down, she felt quite dizzy. Her hands shook, and the tree shook too. If she slipped now, there was only one direction in which she could fall—down, down, into the depths of that dark and shadowy ravine.

There was only one thing to do; concentrate on the patch of blue just a couple of feet away from her.

She did not look down or up, but straight ahead, and willing herself forward, she managed to reach the umbrella.

She could not crawl back with it in her hands. So, after dislodging it from the forked branch in which it had stuck, she let it fall, still open, into the ravine below. Cushioned by the wind, the umbrella floated serenely downwards, landing in a thicket of nettles.

Binya crawled back along the trunk of the cherry tree.

Twenty minutes later, she emerged from the nettle clump, her precious umbrella held aloft. She had nettle stings all over her legs, but she was hardly aware of the smarting. She was as immune to nettles as Bijju was to bees.

3

About four years previously, Bijju had knocked a hive out of an oak tree, and had been badly stung on the face and legs. It had been a painful experience. But now, if a bee stung him, he felt nothing at all: he had been immunized for life!

He was on his way home from school. It was two o'clock and he hadn't eaten since six in the morning. Fortunately, the Kingora bushes—the bilberries—were in fruit, and already Bijju's lips were stained purple with the juice of the wild, sour fruit.

He didn't have any money to spend at Ram Bharosa's shop, but he stopped there anyway to look at the sweets in their glass jars.

'And what will you have today?' asked Ram Bharosa.

'No money,' said Bijju.

'You can pay me later.'

Bijju shook his head. Some of his friends had taken sweets on credit, and at the end of the month they had found they'd eaten more sweets than they could possibly pay for! As a result, they'd had to hand over to Ram Bharosa some of their most treasured possessions—such as a curved knife for cutting grass, or a small hand-axe, or a jar for pickles, or a pair of earrings—and these had become the shopkeeper's possessions and were kept by him or sold in his shop.

Ram Bharosa had set his heart on having Binya's blue umbrella, and so naturally he was anxious to give credit to either of the children, but so far neither had fallen into the trap.

Bijju moved on, his mouth full of Kingora berries. Halfway home, he saw Binya with the cows. It was late evening, and the sun had gone down, but Binya still had the umbrella open. The two small rents had been stitched up by her mother.

Bijju gave his sister a handful of berries. She handed him the umbrella while she ate the berries.

'You can have the umbrella until we get home,' she said. It was her way of rewarding Bijju for bringing her the wild fruit.

Calling, 'Neelu! Gori!', Binya and Bijju set out for home,

followed at some distance by the cows.

It was dark before they reached the village, but Bijju still had the umbrella open.

◆

Most of the people in the village were a little envious of Binya's blue umbrella. No one else had ever possessed one like it. The schoolmaster's wife thought it was quite wrong for a poor cultivator's daughter to have such a fine umbrella while she, a second-class BA, had to make do with an ordinary black one. Her husband offered to have their old umbrella dyed blue; she gave him a scornful look, and loved him a little less than before. The pujari, who looked after the temple, announced that he would buy a multicoloured umbrella the next time he was in the town. A few days later he returned looking annoyed and grumbling that they weren't available except in Delhi. Most people consoled themselves by saying that Binya's pretty umbrella wouldn't keep out the rain, if it rained heavily; that it would shrivel in the sun, if the sun was fierce; that it would collapse in a wind, if the wind was strong; that it would attract lightning, if lightning fell near it; and that it would prove unlucky, if there was any ill luck going about. Secretly, everyone admired it.

Unlike the adults, the children didn't have to pretend. They were full of praise for the umbrella. It was so light, so pretty, so bright a blue! And it was just the right size for Binya. They knew that if they said nice things about the umbrella, Binya would smile and give it to them to hold for a little while—just a very little while!

Soon it was the time of the monsoon. Big black clouds kept piling up, and thunder rolled over the hills.

Binya sat on the hillside all afternoon, waiting for the rain.

As soon as the first big drop of rain came down, she raised the umbrella over her head. More drops, big ones, came pattering down. She could see them through the umbrella silk, as they broke against the cloth.

And then there was a cloudburst, and it was like standing under a waterfall. The umbrella wasn't really a rain umbrella, but it held up bravely. Only Binya's feet got wet. Rods of rain fell around her in a curtain of shivered glass.

Everywhere on the hillside people were scurrying for shelter. Some made for a charcoal burner's hut, others for a mule-shed, or Ram Bharosa's shop. Binya was the only one who didn't run. This was what she'd been waiting for—rain on her umbrella—and she wasn't in a hurry to go home. She didn't mind getting her feet wet. The cows didn't mind getting wet either.

Presently she found Bijju sheltering in a cave. He would have enjoyed getting wet, but he had his schoolbooks with him and he couldn't afford to let them get spoilt. When he saw Binya, he came out of the cave and shared the umbrella. He was a head taller than his sister, so he had to hold the umbrella for her, while she held his books.

The cows had been left far behind.

'Neelu, Neelu!' called Binya.

'Gori!' called Bijju.

When their mother saw them sauntering home through the driving rain, she called out: 'Binya! Bijju! Hurry up and bring the cows in! What are you doing out there in the rain?'

'Just testing the umbrella,' said Bijju.

4

The rains set in, and the sun only made brief appearances. The hills turned a lush green. Ferns sprang up on walls and tree trunks. Giant lilies reared up like leopards from the tall grass. A white mist coiled and uncoiled as it floated up from the valley. It was a beautiful season, except for the leeches.

Every day, Binya came home with a couple of leeches fastened to the flesh of her bare legs. They fell off by themselves just as soon as they'd had their thimbleful of blood, but you didn't know they were on you until they fell off, and then, later, the skin became very sore and itchy. Some of the older people still believed that to be bled by leeches was a remedy for various ailments. Whenever Ram Bharosa had a headache, he applied a leech to his throbbing temple.

Three days of incessant rain had flooded out a number of small animals who lived in holes in the ground. Binya's mother suddenly found the roof full of field rats. She had to drive them out; they ate too much of her stored-up wheat flour and rice. Bijju liked lifting up large rocks to disturb the scorpions who were sleeping beneath. And snakes came out to bask in the sun.

Binya had just crossed the small stream at the bottom of the hill when she saw something gliding out of the bushes and coming towards her. It was a long black snake. A clatter of loose stones frightened it. Seeing the girl in its way, it rose up, hissing, prepared to strike. The forked tongue darted out, the venomous head lunged at Binya.

Binya's umbrella was open as usual. She thrust it forward, between herself and the snake, and the snake's hard snout thudded twice against the strong silk of the umbrella. The reptile then turned and slithered away over the wet rocks, disappearing into a clump of ferns.

Binya forgot about the cows and ran all the way home to tell her mother how she had been saved by the umbrella. Bijju had to put away his books and go out to fetch the cows. He carried a stout stick, in case he met with any snakes.

◆

First the summer sun, and now the endless rain, meant that the umbrella was beginning to fade a little. From a bright blue it had changed to a light blue. But it was still a pretty thing, and tougher than it looked, and Ram Bharosa still desired it. He did not want to sell it; he wanted to own it. He was probably the richest man in the area—so why shouldn't he have a blue umbrella? Not a day passed without his getting a glimpse of Binya and the umbrella; and the more he saw the umbrella, the more he wanted it.

The schools closed during the monsoon, but this didn't mean that Bijju could sit at home doing nothing. Neelu and Gori were providing more milk than was required at home, so Binya's mother was able to sell a kilo of milk every day: half a kilo to the schoolmaster, and half a kilo (at reduced rate) to the temple pujari. Bijju had to deliver the milk every morning.

Ram Bharosa had asked Bijju to work in his shop during the holidays, but Bijju didn't have time—he had to help his mother with the ploughing and the transplanting of the rice seedlings. So Ram Bharosa employed a boy from the next village, a boy called Rajaram. He did all the washing-up, and ran various errands. He went to the same school as Bijju, but the two boys were not friends.

One day, as Binya passed the shop, twirling her blue umbrella, Rajaram noticed that his employer gave a deep sigh and began muttering to himself.

'What's the matter, Babuji?' asked the boy.

'Oh, nothing,' said Ram Bharosa. 'It's just a sickness that has come upon me. And it's all due to that girl Binya and her wretched umbrella.'

'Why, what has she done to you?'

'Refused to sell me her umbrella! There's pride for you. And I offered her ten rupees.'

'Perhaps, if you gave her twelve...'

'But it isn't new any longer. It isn't worth eight rupees now. All the same, I'd like to have it.'

'You wouldn't make a profit on it,' said Rajaram.

'It's not the profit I'm after, wretch! It's the thing itself. It's the beauty of it!'

'And what would you do with it, Babuji? You don't visit anyone—you're seldom out of your shop. Of what use would it be to you?'

'Of what use is a poppy in a cornfield? Of what use is a rainbow? Of what use are you, numbskull? Wretch! I, too, have a soul. I want the umbrella, because—because I want its beauty to be mine!'

Rajaram put the kettle on to boil, began dusting the counter, all the time muttering: 'I'm as useful as an umbrella,' and then, after a short period of intense thought, said: 'What will you give me, Babuji, if I get the umbrella for you?'

'What do you mean?' asked the old man.

'You know what I mean. What will you give me?'

'You mean to steal it, don't you, you wretch? What a delightful child you are! I'm glad you're not my son or my enemy. But look, everyone will know it has been stolen, and then how will I be able to show off with it?'

'You will have to gaze upon it in secret,' said Rajaram with a chuckle. 'Or take it into Tehri, and have it coloured red! That's your problem. But tell me, Babuji, do you want it badly enough to pay me three rupees for stealing it without being seen?'

Ram Bharosa gave the boy a long, sad look. 'You're a sharp boy,' he said. 'You'll come to a bad end. I'll give you two rupees.'

'Three,' said the boy.

'Two,' said the old man.

'You don't really want it, I can see that,' said the boy.

'Wretch!' said the old man. 'Evil one! Darkener of my doorstep! Fetch me the umbrella, and I'll give you three rupees.'

5

Binya was in the forest glade where she had first seen the umbrella. No one came there for picnics during the monsoon. The grass was always wet and the pine needles were slippery underfoot. The tall trees shut out the light, and poisonous-looking mushrooms, orange and purple, sprang up everywhere. But it was a good place for porcupines, who seemed to like the mushrooms, and Binya was searching for porcupine quills.

The hill people didn't think much of porcupine quills, but far away in southern India, the quills were valued as charms and sold at a rupee each. So Ram Bharosa paid a tenth of a rupee for each quill brought to him, and he in turn sold the quills at a profit to a trader from the plains.

Binya had already found five quills, and she knew there'd be more in the long grass. For once, she'd put her umbrella down. She had to put it aside if she was to search the ground thoroughly.

It was Rajaram's chance.

He'd been following Binya for some time, concealing himself behind trees and rocks, creeping closer whenever she became absorbed in her search. He was anxious that she should not see him and be able to recognize him later.

He waited until Binya had wandered some distance from

the umbrella. Then, running forward at a crouch, he seized the open umbrella and dashed off with it.

But Rajaram had very big feet. Binya heard his heavy footsteps and turned just in tune to see him as he disappeared between the trees. She cried out, dropped the porcupine quills, and gave chase.

Binya was swift and sure-footed, but Rajaram had a long stride. All the same, he made the mistake of running downhill. A long-legged person is much faster going up hill than down. Binya reached the edge of the forest glade in time to see the thief scrambling down the path to the stream. He had closed the umbrella so that it would not hinder his flight.

Binya was beginning to gain on the boy. He kept to the path, while she simply slid and leapt down the steep hillside. Near the bottom of the hill the path began to straighten out, and it was here that the long-legged boy began to forge ahead again.

Bijju was coming home from another direction. He had a bundle of sticks which he'd collected for the kitchen fire. As he reached the path, he saw Binya rushing down the hill as though all the mountain spirits in Garhwal were after her.

'What's wrong?' he called. 'Why are you running?'

Binya paused only to point at the fleeing Rajaram.

'My umbrella!' she cried. 'He has stolen it!'

Bijju dropped his bundle of sticks, and ran after his sister. When he reached her side, he said, 'I'll soon catch him!' and went sprinting away over the lush green grass. He was fresh, and he was soon well ahead of Binya and gaining on the thief.

Rajaram was crossing the shallow stream when Bijju caught up with him. Rajaram was the taller boy, but Bijju was much stronger. He flung himself at the thief, caught him by the legs, and brought him down in the water. Rajaram got to his feet and tried to drag himself away, but Bijju still had him by a leg. Rajaram overbalanced and came down with a great splash. He had let the umbrella fall. It began to float away on the current. Just then Binya arrived, flushed and breathless, and went dashing into the stream after the umbrella.

Meanwhile, a tremendous fight was taking place. Locked in fierce combat, the two boys swayed together on a rock, tumbled on to the sand, rolled over and over the pebbled bank until they were again thrashing about in the shallows of the stream. The magpies, bulbuls and other birds were disturbed, and flew away with cries of alarm.

Covered with mud, gasping and spluttering, the boys groped for each other in the water. After five minutes of frenzied struggle, Bijju emerged victorious. Rajaram lay flat on his back on the sand, exhausted, while Bijju sat astride him, pinning him down with his arms and legs.

'Let me get up!' gasped Rajaram. 'Let me go—I don't want your useless umbrella!'

'Then why did you take it?' demanded Bijju. 'Come on—tell me why!'

'It was that skinflint Ram Bharosa,' said Rajaram. 'He told me to get it for him. He said if I didn't fetch it, I'd lose my job.'

6

By early October, the rains were coming to an end. The leeches disappeared. The ferns turned yellow, and the sunlight on the green hills was mellow and golden, like the limes on the small tree in front of Binya's home. Bijju's days were happy ones as he came home from school, munching on roasted corn. Binya's umbrella had turned a pale milky blue, and was patched in several places, but it was still the prettiest umbrella in the village, and she still carried it with her wherever she went.

The cold, cruel winter wasn't far off, but somehow October seems longer than other months, because it is a kind month: the grass is good to be upon, the breeze is warm and gentle and pine-scented. That October, everyone seemed contented—everyone, that is, except Ram Bharosa.

The old man had by now given up all hope of ever possessing Binya's umbrella. He wished he had never set eyes on it. Because of the umbrella, he had suffered the tortures of greed, the despair of loneliness. Because of the umbrella, people had stopped coming to his shop!

Ever since it had become known that Ram Bharosa had tried to have the umbrella stolen, the village people had turned against him. They stopped trusting the old man; instead of buying their soap and tea and matches from his shop, they preferred to walk an extra mile to the shops near the Tehri bus stand. Who would have dealings with a man who had sold his soul for an umbrella? The children taunted him, twisted his name around. From 'Ram the Trustworthy' he became 'Trusty Umbrella Thief'.

The old man sat alone in his empty shop, listening to the eternal hissing of his kettle and wondering if anyone would ever again step in for a glass of tea. Ram Bharosa had lost his own appetite, and ate and drank very little. There was no money coming in. He had his savings in a bank in Tehri, but it was a terrible thing to have to dip into them! To save money, he had dismissed the blundering Rajaram. So he was left without any company. The roof leaked and the wind got in through the corrugated tin sheets, but Ram Bharosa didn't care.

Bijju and Binya passed his shop almost every day. Bijju went by with a loud but tuneless whistle. He was one of the world's whistlers; cares rested lightly on his shoulders. But, strangely enough, Binya crept quietly past the shop, looking the other way, almost as though she was in some way responsible for the misery of Ram Bharosa.

She kept reasoning with herself, telling herself that the umbrella was her very own, and that she couldn't help it if others were jealous of it. But had she loved the umbrella too much? Had it mattered more to her than people mattered? She couldn't help feeling that, in a small way, she was the cause of the sad look on Ram Bharosa's face ('His face is a yard long,' said Bijju) and the ruinous condition of his shop. It was all due to his own greed, no doubt, but she didn't want him to feel too bad about what he'd done, because it made her feel bad about herself; and so she closed the umbrella whenever she came near the shop, opening it again only when she was out of sight.

One day towards the end of October, when she had ten paise in her pocket, she entered the shop and asked the old man for a toffee.

She was Ram Bharosa's first customer in almost two weeks. He looked suspiciously at the girl. Had she come to taunt him, to flaunt the umbrella in his face? She had placed her coin on the counter. Perhaps it was a bad coin. Ram Bharosa picked it up and bit it; he held it up to the light; he rang it on the ground. It was a good coin. He gave Binya the toffee.

Binya had already left the shop when Ram Bharosa saw the closed umbrella lying on his counter. There it was, the blue umbrella he had always wanted, within his grasp at last! He had only to hide it at the back of his shop, and no one would know that he had it, no one could prove that Binya had left it behind.

He stretched out his trembling, bony hand, and took the umbrella by the handle. He pressed it open. He stood beneath it, in the dark shadows of his shop, where no sun or rain could ever touch it.

'But I'm never in the sun or in the rain,' he said aloud. 'Of what use is an umbrella to me?'

And he hurried outside and ran after Binya.

'Binya, Binya!' he shouted. 'Binya, you've left your umbrella behind!'

He wasn't used to running, but he caught up with her, held out the umbrella, saying, 'You forgot it—the umbrella!'

In that moment it belonged to both of them.

But Binya didn't take the umbrella. She shook her head and said, 'You keep it. I don't need it any more.'

'But it's such a pretty umbrella!' protested Ram Bharosa. 'It's the best umbrella in the village.'

'I know,' said Binya. 'But an umbrella isn't everything.'

And she left the old man holding the umbrella, and went tripping down the road, and there was nothing between her and the bright blue sky.

7

Well, now that Ram Bharosa has the blue umbrella—a gift from Binya, as he tells everyone—he is sometimes persuaded to go out into the sun or the rain, and as a result he looks much healthier. Sometimes he uses the umbrella to chase away pigs or goats. It is always left open outside the shop, and anyone who wants to borrow it may do so; and so in a way it has become everyone's umbrella. It is faded and patchy, but it is still the best umbrella in the village.

People are visiting Ram Bharosa's shop again. Whenever

Bijju or Binya stop for a cup of tea, he gives them a little extra milk or sugar. They like their tea sweet and milky.

A few nights ago, a bear visited Ram Bharosa's shop. There had been snow on the higher ranges of the Himalayas, and the bear had been finding it difficult to obtain food; so it had come lower down, to see what it could pick up near the village. That night it scrambled on to the tin roof of Ram Bharosa's shop, and made off with a huge pumpkin which had been ripening on the roof. But in climbing off the roof, the bear had lost a claw.

Next morning Ram Bharosa found the claw just outside the door of his shop. He picked it up and put it in his pocket. A bear's claw was a lucky find.

A day later, when he went into the market town, he took the claw with him, and left it with a silversmith, giving the craftsman certain instructions.

The silversmith made a locket for the claw, then he gave it a thin silver chain. When Ram Bharosa came again, he paid the silversmith ten rupees for his work.

The days were growing shorter, and Binya had to be home a little earlier every evening. There was a hungry leopard at large, and she couldn't leave the cows out after dark.

She was hurrying past Ram Bharosa's shop when the old man called out to her.

'Binya, spare a minute! I want to show you something.'

Binya stepped into the shop.

'What do you think of it?' asked Ram Bharosa, showing her the silver pendant with the claw.

'It's so beautiful,' said Binya, just touching the claw and the silver chain.

'It's a bear's claw,' said Ram Bharosa. 'That's even luckier than a leopard's claw. Would you like to have it?'

'I have no money,' said Binya.

'That doesn't matter. You gave me the umbrella, I give you the claw! Come, let's see what it looks like on you.'

He placed the pendant on Binya, and indeed it looked very beautiful on her.

Ram Bharosa says he will never forget the smile she gave him when she left the shop.

She was halfway home when she realized she had left the cows behind.

'Neelu, Neelu!' she called. 'Oh, Gori!'

There was a faint tinkle of bells as the cows came slowly down the mountain path.

In the distance she could hear her mother and Bijju calling for her.

She began to sing. They heard her singing, and knew she was safe and near.

She walked home through the darkening glade, singing of the stars, and the trees stood still and listened to her, and the mountains were glad.

The Eyes of the Eagle

IT WAS A HIGH, PIERCING SOUND, ALMOST LIKE THE YELPING OF A dog. Jai stopped picking the wild strawberries that grew in the grass around him, and looked up at the sky. He had a dog—a shaggy guard-dog called Motu—but Motu did not yet yelp, he growled and barked. The strange sound came from the sky, and Jai had heard it before. Now, realising what it was, he jumped to his feet, calling to his dog, calling his sheep to start for home. Motu came bounding towards him, ready for a game.

'Not now, Motu!' said Jai. 'We must get the lambs home quickly.' Again he looked up at the sky.

He saw it now, a black speck against the sun, growing larger as it circled the mountain, coming lower every moment—a Golden Eagle, king of the skies over the higher Himalayas, ready now to swoop and seize its prey.

Had it seen a pheasant or a pine marten? Or was it after one of the lambs? Jai had never lost a lamb to an eagle, but recently some of the other shepherds had been talking about a golden eagle that had been preying on their flocks.

The sheep had wandered some way down the side of the

mountain, and Jai ran after them to make sure that none of the lambs had gone off on its own.

Motu ran about, barking furiously. He wasn't very good at keeping the sheep together—he was often bumping into them and sending them tumbling down the slope—but his size and bear-like look kept the leopards and wolves at a distance.

Jai was counting the lambs; they were bleating loudly and staying close to their mothers. *One—two—three—four…*

There should have been a fifth. Jai couldn't see it on the slope below him. He looked up towards a rocky ledge near the steep path to the Tung temple. The golden eagle was circling the rocks.

The bird disappeared from sight for a moment, then rose again with a small creature grasped firmly in its terrible talons.

'It has taken a lamb!' shouted Jai. He started scrambling up the slope. Motu ran ahead of him, barking furiously at the big bird as it glided away over the tops of the stunted junipers to its eyrie on the cliffs above Tung.

There was nothing that Jai and Motu could do except stare helplessly and angrily at the disappearing eagle. The lamb had died the instant it had been struck. The rest of the flock seemed unaware of what had happened. They still grazed on the thick, sweet grass of the mountain slopes.

'We had better drive them home, Motu,' said Jai, and at a nod from the boy, the big dog bounded down the slope, to take part in his favourite game of driving the sheep homewards. Soon he had them running all over the place, and Jai had to dash about trying to keep them together. Finally they straggled homewards.

'A fine lamb gone,' said Jai to himself gloomily. 'I wonder what Grandfather will say.'

Grandfather said, 'Never mind. It had to happen some day. That eagle has been watching the sheep for some time.'

Grandmother, more practical, said; 'We could have sold the lamb for three hundred rupees. You'll have to be more careful in future, Jai. Don't fall asleep on the hillside, and don't read storybooks when you are supposed to be watching the sheep!'

'I wasn't reading this morning,' said Jai truthfully, forgetting to mention that he had been gathering strawberries.

'It's good for him to read,' said Grandfather, who had never had the luck to go to school. In his days, there weren't any schools in the mountains. Now there was one in every village.

'Time enough to read at night,' said Grandmother, who did not think much of the little one-room school down at Maku, their home village.

'Well, these are the October holidays,' said Grandfather. 'Otherwise he would not be here to help us with the sheep. It will snow by the end of the month, and then we will move with the flock. You will have more time for reading then, Jai.'

◆

At Maku, which was down in the warmer valley, Jai's parents tilled a few narrow terraces on which they grew barley, millets and potatoes. The old people brought their sheep up to the Tung meadows to graze during the summer months. They stayed in a small stone hut just off the path which pilgrims took to the ancient temple. At twelve thousand feet above sea level, it was the highest Hindu temple on the inner Himalayan ranges.

The following day Jai and Motu were very careful. The did not let the sheep out of sight even for a minute. Nor did they catch sight of the golden eagle. 'What if it attacks again?' wondered Jai. 'How will I stop it?'

The great eagle, with its powerful beak and talons, was more than a match for boy or dog. Its hind claw, four inches round the curve, was its most dangerous weapon. When it spread its wings, the distance from tip to tip was more than eight feet.

The eagle did not come that day because it had fed well and was now resting in its eyrie. Old bones, which had belonged to pheasants, snow-cocks, pine martens and even foxes, were scattered about the rocks which formed the eagle's home. The eagle had a mate, but it was not the breeding season and she was away on a scouting expedition of her own.

The golden eagle stood on its rocky ledge, staring majestically across the valley. Its hard, unblinking eyes missed nothing. Those strange orange-yellow eyes could spot a field-rat or a mouse-hare more than a hundred yards below.

There were other eagles on the mountain, but usually they kept to their own territory. And only the bolder ones went for lambs, because the flocks were always protected by men and dogs.

The eagle took off from its eyrie and glided gracefully, powerfully over the valley, circling the Tung mountain.

Below lay the old temple, built from slabs of grey granite. A line of pilgrims snaked up the steep, narrow path. On the meadows below the peak, the sheep grazed peacefully, unaware of the presence of the eagle. The great bird's shadow slid over the sunlit slopes.

The eagle saw the boy and the dog, but he did not fear them. He had his eye on a lamb that was frisking about on the grass, a few feet away from the other grazing sheep.

Jai did not see the eagle until it swept round an outcrop of rocks about a hundred feet away. It moved silently, without any movement of its wings, for it had already built up the momentum for its dive. Now it came straight at the lamb.

Motu saw the bird in time. With a low growl he dashed forward and reached the side of the lamb at almost the same instant that the eagle swept in.

There was a terrific collision. Feathers flew. The eagle screamed with rage. The lamb tumbled down the slope, and Motu howled in pain as the huge beak struck him high on the leg.

The big bird, a little stunned by the clash, flew off rather unsteadily, with a mighty beating of its wings.

Motu had saved the lamb. It was frightened but unhurt. Bleating loudly, it joined the other sheep, who took up the bleating. Jai ran up to Motu, who lay whimpering on the ground. There was no sign of the eagle. Quickly he removed his shirt and vest; then he wrapped his vest round the dog's wound, tying it in position with his belt.

Motu could not get up, and he was much too heavy for Jai to carry. Jai did not want to leave his dog alone, in case the eagle returned to attack.

He stood up, cupped his hand to his mouth, and began calling for his grandfather.

'Dada, dada!' he shouted, and presently Grandfather heard him and came stumbling down the slope. He was followed by another shepherd, and together they lifted Motu and carried him home.

Motu had a bad wound, but Grandmother cleaned it and applied a paste made of herbs. Then she laid strips of carrot over the wound—an old mountain remedy—and bandaged the leg. But it would be some time before Motu could run about again. By then it would probably be snowing and time to leave these high-altitude pastures and return to the valley. Meanwhile, the sheep had to be taken out to graze, and Grandfather decided to accompany Jai for the remaining period.

They did not see the golden eagle for two or three days, and, when they did, it was flying over the next range. Perhaps it had found some other source of food, or even another flock of sheep. 'Are you afraid of the eagle?' Grandfather asked Jai.

'I wasn't before,' said Jai. 'Not until it hurt Motu. I did not know it could be so dangerous. But Motu hurt it too. He banged straight into it!'

'Perhaps it won't bother us again,' said Grandfather thoughtfully. 'A bird's wing is easily injured—even an eagle's.'

Jai wasn't so sure. He had seen it strike twice, and he knew that it was not afraid of anyone. Only when it learnt to fear his presence would it keep away from the flock.

The next day Grandfather did not feel well; he was feverish and kept to his bed. Motu was hobbling about gamely on three legs; the wounded leg was still very sore.

'Don't go too far with the sheep,' said Grandmother. 'Let them graze near the house.'

'But there's hardly any grass here,' said Jai.

'I don't want you wandering off while that eagle is still around.'

'Give him my stick,' said Grandfather from his bed. Grandmother took it from the corner and handed it to the boy.

It was an old stick, made of wild cherrywood, which Grandfather often carried around. The wood was strong and well-seasoned; the stick was stout and long. It reached up to Jai's shoulders.

'Don't lose it,' said Grandfather. 'It was given to me many years ago by a wandering scholar who came to the Tung temple. I was going to give it to you when you got bigger, but perhaps this is the right time for you to have it. If the eagle comes near you, swing the stick around your head. That should frighten it off!'

Clouds had gathered over the mountains, and a heavy mist hid the Tung temple. With the approach of winter, the flow of pilgrims had been reduced to a trickle. The shepherds had started leaving the lush meadows and returning to their villages at lower altitudes. Very soon the bears and the leopards and the golden eagles would have the high ranges all to themselves.

Jai used the cherrywood stick to prod the sheep along the path until they reached the steep meadows. The stick would have to be a substitute for Motu. And they seemed to respond to it more readily than they did to Motu's mad charges.

Because of the sudden cold and the prospect of snow, Grandmother had made Jai wear a rough woollen jacket and a pair of high boots bought from a Tibetan trader. He wasn't used to the boots—he wore sandals at other times—and had some difficulty in climbing quickly up and down the hillside. It was tiring work, trying to keep the flock together. The cawing of some crows warned Jai that the eagle might be around, but the mist prevented him from seeing very far.

After some time the mist lifted and Jai was able to see the temple and the snow peaks towering behind it. He saw the golden eagle, too. It was circling high overhead. Jai kept close to the flock—one eye on the eagle, one eye on the restless sheep.

Then the great bird stooped and flew lower. It circled the temple and then pretended to go away. Jai felt sure it would be back. And a few minutes later it reappeared from the other side of the mountain. It was much lower now, wings spread out and back, taloned feet to the fore, piercing eyes fixed on its target—a small lamb that had suddenly gone frisking down the slope, away from Jai and the flock.

Now it flew lower still, only a few feet off the ground, paying no attention to the boy.

It passed Jai with a great rush of air, and as it did so the boy struck out with his stick and caught the bird a glancing blow.

The eagle missed its prey, and the tiny lamb skipped away.

To Jai's amazement, the bird did not fly off. Instead it landed on the hillside and glared at the boy, as a king would glare at a humble subject who had dared to pelt him with a pebble.

The golden eagle stood almost as tall as Jai. Its wings were still outspread. Its fierce eyes seemed to be looking through and through the boy.

Jai's first instinct was to turn and run. But the cherrywood stick was still in his hands, and he felt sure there was power in it. He saw that the eagle was about to launch itself again at the lamb. Instead of running away, he ran forward, the stick raised above his head.

The eagle rose a few feet off the ground and struck out with its huge claws.

Luckily for Jai, his heavy jacket took the force of the blow. A talon ripped through the sleeve, and the sleeve fell away. At the same time the heavy stick caught the eagle across its open wing. The bird gave a shrill cry of pain and fury. Then it turned and flapped heavily away, flying unsteadily because of its injured wing.

Jai still clutched the stick, because he expected the bird to return; he did not even glance at his torn jacket. But the golden eagle had alighted on a distant rock and was in no hurry to return to the attack.

Jai began driving the sheep home. The clouds had become heavy and black, and presently the first snowflakes began to fall.

Jai saw a hare go lolloping done the hill. When it was about fifty yards away, there was a rush of air from the eagle's beating wings, and Jai saw the bird approaching the hare in a sidelong drive.

'So it hasn't been badly hurt,' thought Jai, feeling a little relieved, for he could not help admiring the great bird. 'Now it has found something else to chase for its dinner.'

The hare saw the eagle and dodged about, making for a clump of junipers. Jai did not know if it was caught or not, because the snow and sleet had increased and both bird and hare were lost in the gathering snowstorm.

The sheep were bleating behind him. One of the lambs looked tired, and he stooped to pick it up. As he did so, he heard a thin, whining sound. It grew louder by the second. Before he could look up, a huge wing caught him across the shoulders and sent him sprawling. The lamb tumbled down the slope with him, into a thorny bilberry bush.

The bush saved them. Jai saw the eagle coming in again, flying low. It was another eagle! One had been vanquished, and now here was another, just as big and fearless, probably the mate of the first eagle.

Jai had lost his stick and there was no way by which he could fight the second eagle. So he crept further into the bush, holding the lamb beneath him. At the same time he began shouting at the top of his voice—both to scare the bird away and to summon help. The eagle could not easily get at them now; but the rest of the flock was exposed on the hillside. Surely the eagle would make for them.

Even as the bird circled and came back in another dive, Jai heard fierce barking. The eagle immediately swung away and rose skywards.

The barking came from Motu. Hearing Jai's shouts and sensing that something was wrong, he had come limping out of the house, ready to do battle. Behind him came another shepherd and—most wonderful of all—Grandmother herself, banging two frying pans together. The barking, the banging and the shouting frightened the eagles away. The sheep scattered too, and it was some time before they could all be rounded up. By then it was snowing heavily.

'Tomorrow we must all go down to Maku,' said the shepherd.

'Yes, it's time we went,' said Grandmother. 'You can read your storybooks again, Jai.'

'I'll have my own story to tell,' said Jai.

When they reached the hut and Jai saw Grandfather, he said, 'Oh, I've forgotten your stick!'

But Motu had picked it up. Carrying it between his teeth, he brought it home and sat down with it in the open doorway. He had decided the cherrywood was good for his teeth and would have chewed it up if Grandmother hadn't taken it from him.

'Never mind,' said Grandfather, sitting up on his cot. 'It isn't the stick that matters. It's the person who holds it.'

From Small Beginnings

And the last puff of the day-wind brought from the unseen villages the scent of damp wood-smoke, hot cakes, dripping undergrowth, and rotting pine-cones. That is the true smell of the Himalayas, and if once it creeps into the blood of a man, that man will at the last, forgetting all else, return to the hills to die.

—Rudyard Kipling

ON THE FIRST CLEAR SEPTEMBER DAY, TOWARDS THE END OF THE rains, I visited the pine knoll, my place of peace and power.

It was months since I'd last been there. Trips to the plains, a crisis in my affairs, involvements with other people and their troubles, and an entire monsoon had come between me and the grassy, pine-topped slope facing the Hill of Fairies (Pari Tibba to the locals). Now I tramped through late monsoon foliage—tall ferns, bushes festooned with flowering convolvulus—and crossed the stream by way of its little bridge of stones before climbing the steep hill to the pine slope.

When the trees saw me, they made as if to turn in my

direction. A puff of wind came across the valley from the distant snows. A long-tailed blue magpie took alarm and flew noisily out of an oak tree. The cicadas were suddenly silent. But the trees remembered me. They bowed gently in the breeze and beckoned me nearer, welcoming me home. Three pines, a straggling oak and a wild cherry. I went among them and acknowledged their welcome with a touch of my hand against their trunks—the cherry's smooth and polished; the pine's patterned and whorled; the oak's rough, gnarled, full of experience. He'd been there longest, and the wind had bent his upper branches and twisted a few, so that he looked shaggy and undistinguished. But like the philosopher who is careless about his dress and appearance, the oak has secrets, a hidden wisdom. He has learnt the art of survival!

While the oak and the pines are older than me and have been here many years, the cherry tree is exactly seven years old. I know, because I planted it.

One day I had this cherry seed in my hand, and on an impulse I thrust it into the soft earth, and then went away and forgot all about it. A few months later I found a tiny cherry tree in the long grass. I did not expect it to survive. But the following year it was two feet tall. And then some goats ate its leaves and a grass cutter's scythe injured the stem, and I was sure it would wither away. But it renewed itself, sprang up even faster, and within three years it was a healthy, growing tree, about five feet tall.

I left the hills for two years—forced by circumstances to make a living in Delhi—but this time I did not forget the cherry tree. I thought about it fairly often, sent telepathic messages of encouragement in its direction. And when, a couple of years ago, I returned in the autumn, my heart did a somersault when I found my tree sprinkled with pale pink blossom. (The Himalayan cherry flowers in November.) And later, when the fruit was ripe, the tree was visited by finches, tits, bulbuls and other small birds, all come to feast on the sour, red cherries.

Last summer I spent a night on the pine knoll, sleeping on the grass beneath the cherry tree. I lay awake for hours, listening to the chatter of the stream and the occasional *tonk-tonk* of nightjars, and watching through the branches overhead, the stars turning in the sky. And I felt the power of the sky and the earth, and the power of a small cherry seed...

And so when the rains are over, this is where I come, that I might feel the peace and power of this place.

This is where I will write my stories. I can see everything from here—my cottage across the valley; behind and above me, the town and the bazaar, straddling the ridge; to the left, the high mountains and the twisting road to the source of the great river; below me, the little stream and the path to the village; ahead, the Hill of Fairies and the fields beyond; the wide valley below, and another range of hills and then the distant plains. I can even see Prem Singh in the garden, putting the mattresses out in the sun.

From here he is just a speck on the far hill, but I know it is Prem by the way he stands. A man may have a hundred disguises, but in the end it is his posture that gives him away. Like my grandfather, who was a master of disguise and successfully roamed the bazaars as fruit vendor or basket maker. But we could always recognize him because of his pronounced slouch.

Prem Singh doesn't slouch, but he has this habit of looking up at the sky (regardless of whether it's cloudy or clear), and at the moment he's looking at the sky.

Eight years with Prem. He was just a sixteen-year-old boy

when I first saw him, and now he has a wife and child.

I had been in the cottage for just over a year… He stood on the landing outside the kitchen door. A tall boy, dark, with good teeth and brown, deep-set eyes, dressed smartly in white drill—his only change of clothes. Looking for a job. I liked the look of him, but—

'I already have someone working for me,' I said.

'Yes, sir. He is my uncle.'

In the hills, everyone is a brother or an uncle.

'You don't want me to dismiss your uncle?'

'No, sir. But he says you can find a job for me.'

'I'll try. I'll make inquiries. Have you just come from your village?'

'Yes. Yesterday I walked ten miles to Pauri. There I got a bus.'

'Sit down. Your uncle will make some tea.'

He sat down on the steps, removed his white keds, wriggled his toes. His feet were both long and broad, large feet but not ugly. He was unusually clean for a hill boy. And taller than most.

'Do you smoke?' I asked.

'No, sir.'

'It is true,' said his uncle. 'He does not smoke. All my nephews smoke but this one. He is a little peculiar, he does not smoke—neither beedi nor hookah.'

'Do you drink?'

'It makes me vomit.'

'Do you take bhang?'

'No, sahib.'

'You have no vices. It's unnatural.'

'He is unnatural, sahib,' said his uncle.

'Does he chase girls?'

'They chase him, sahib.'

'So he left the village and came looking for a job.' I looked at him. He grinned, then looked away and began rubbing his feet.

'Your name is...?'

'Prem Singh.'

'All right, Prem, I will try to do something for you.'

I did not see him for a couple of weeks. I forgot about finding him a job. But when I met him again, on the road to the bazaar, he told me that he had got a temporary job in the Survey, looking after the surveyor's tents.

'Next week we will be going to Rajasthan,' he said.

'It will be very hot. Have you been in the desert before?'

'No, sir.'

'It is not like the hills. And it is far from home.'

'I know. But I have no choice in the matter. I have to collect some money in order to get married.'

In his region there was a bride price, usually of 2,000 rupees.

'Do you have to get married so soon?'

'I have only one brother and he is still very young. My mother is not well. She needs a daughter-in-law to help her in the fields and the house, and with the cows. We are a small family, so the work is greater.'

Every family has its few terraced fields, narrow and stony, usually perched on a hillside above a stream or river. They grow rice, barley, maize, potatoes—just enough to live on. Even if their produce is sufficient for marketing, the absence of roads makes it difficult to get the produce to the market towns. There is no money to be earned in the villages, and money is needed for clothes, soap, medicines, and for recovering the family jewellery from the moneylenders. So the young men leave their villages to find work, and to find work they must go to the plains. The lucky ones get into the army. Others enter domestic service or take jobs in garages, hotels, wayside tea shops, schools...

In Mussoorie the main attraction is the large number of schools which employ cooks and bearers. But the schools were full when Prem arrived. He'd been to the recruiting centre at Roorkee, hoping to get into the army; but they found a deformity in his right foot, the result of a bone broken when a landslip carried him away one dark monsoon night. He was lucky, he said, that it was only his foot and not his head that had been broken.

He came to the house to inform his uncle about the job and to say goodbye. I thought, another nice person I probably won't see again; another ship passing in the night, the friendly twinkle of its lights soon vanishing in the darkness. I said 'Come again', held his smile with mine so that I could remember him better, and returned to my study and my typewriter. The typewriter is the repository of a writer's loneliness. It stares unsympathetically back at him every day, doing its best to be discouraging. Maybe I'll go back to the old-fashioned quill pen and marble inkstand; then I can feel like a real writer—Balzac or Dickens—scratching away into the endless reaches of the night... Of course, the days and nights are seemingly shorter than they need to be! They must be, otherwise why do we hurry so much and achieve so little, by the standards of the past...

Prem goes, disappears into the vast faceless cities of the plains, and a year slips by, or rather I do, and then here he is again, thinner and darker and still smiling and still looking for a job. I should have known that hillmen don't disappear altogether. The spirit-haunted rocks don't let their people wander too far, lest they lose them forever.

I was able to get him a job in the school. The headmaster's wife needed a cook. I wasn't sure if Prem could cook very well but I sent him along and they said they'd give him a trial. Three days later the headmaster's wife met me on the road and started gushing all over me. She was the type who gushed.

'We're so grateful to you! Thank you for sending me that lovely boy. He's so polite. And he cooks very well. A little too hot for my husband, but otherwise delicious—just delicious! He's a real treasure—a lovely boy.' And she gave me an arch look—the famous look which she used to captivate all the good-looking young prefects who became prefects, it was said, only if she approved of them.

I wasn't sure that she didn't want something more than a cook, and I only hoped that Prem would give every satisfaction.

He looked cheerful enough when he came to see me on his off day.

'How are you getting on?' I asked.

'Lovely,' he said, using his mistress's favourite expression.

'What do you mean—lovely? Do they like your work?'

'The memsahib likes it. She strokes me on the cheek whenever she enters the kitchen. The sahib says nothing. He takes medicine after every meal.'

'Did he always take medicine—or only now that you're doing the cooking?'

'I am not sure. I think he has always been sick.'

He was sleeping in the headmaster's veranda and getting sixty rupees a month. A cook in Delhi got a hundred and sixty. And a cook in Paris or New York got ten times as much. I did not say as much to Prem. He might ask me to get him a job in New York. And that would be the last I saw of him! He, as a cook, might well get a job making curries off-Broadway; I, as a writer, wouldn't get to first base. And only my Uncle Ken knew the secret of how to make a living without actually doing any work. But then, of course, he had four sisters. And each of them was married to a fairly prosperous husband. So Uncle Ken divided his year among them. Three months with Aunt Ruby in Nainital. Three months with Aunt Susie in Kashmir. Three months with my mother (not quite so affluent) in Jamnagar. And three months in the Vet Hospital in Bareilly, where Aunt Mabel ran the hospital for her veterinary husband. In this way he never overstayed his welcome. A sister can look after a brother for just three months at a time and no more. Uncle K had it worked out to perfection.

But I had no sisters and I couldn't live forever on the royalties of a single novel. So I had to write others. So I came to the hills.

The hillmen go to the plains to make a living. I had to come to the hills to try and make mine.

'Prem,' I said, 'why don't you work for me?'

'And what about my uncle?'

'He seems ready to desert me any day. His grandfather is ill, he says, and he wants to go home.'

'His grandfather died last year.'

'That's what I mean—he's getting restless. And I don't mind if he goes. These days he seems to be suffering from a form of sleeping sickness. I have to get up first and make his tea…'

Sitting here under the cherry tree, whose leaves are just beginning to turn yellow, I rest my chin on my knees and gaze across the valley to where Prem moves about in the garden. Looking back over the seven years he has been with me, I recall some of the nicest things about him. They come to me in no particular order—just pieces of cinema—coloured slides slipping across the screen of memory…

Prem rocking his infant son to sleep—crooning to him, passing his large hand gently over the child's curly head—Prem following me down to the police station when I was arrested (on a warrant from Bombay, charging me with writing an allegedly obscene short story!), and waiting outside until I reappeared, his smile, when I found him in Delhi, his large, irrepressible laughter, most in evidence when he was seeing an old Laurel and Hardy movie.

Of course, there were times when he could be infuriating, stubborn, deliberately pig-headed, sending me little notes of resignation—but I never found it difficult to overlook these little acts of self-indulgence. He had brought much love and laughter into my life, and what more could a lonely man ask for?

It was his stubborn streak that limited the length of his stay in the headmaster's household. Mr Good was tolerant enough. But Mrs Good was one of those women who, when they are pleased with you, go out of their way to help, pamper and flatter, but when displeased, become vindictive, going out of their way to harm or destroy. Mrs Good sought power—over her husband, her dog, her favourite pupils, her servant... She had absolute power over the husband and the dog, partial power over her slightly bewildered pupils, and none at all over Prem, who missed the subtleties of her designs upon his soul. He did not respond to her mothering, or to the way in which she tweaked him on the cheeks, brushed against him in the kitchen and made admiring remarks about his looks and physique. Memsahibs, he knew, were not for him. So he kept a stony face and went diligently about his duties. And she felt slighted, put in her place. Her liking turned to dislike. Instead of admiring remarks, she began making disparaging remarks about his looks, his clothes, his manners. She found fault with his cooking. No longer was it 'lovely'. She even accused him of taking away the dog's meat and giving it to a poor family living on the hillside—no more heinous crime could be imagined! Mr Good threatened him with dismissal. So Prem became stubborn. The following day he withheld the dog's food altogether, threw it down the khud where it was seized upon by innumerable strays, and went off to the pictures.

That was the end of his job. 'I'll have to go home now,' he told me. 'I won't get another job in this area. The mem will see to that.'

'Stay a few days,' I said.

'I have only enough money with which to get home.'

'Keep it for going home. You can stay with me for a few days, while you look around. Your uncle won't mind sharing his food with you.'

His uncle did mind. He did not like the idea of working for his nephew as well; it seemed to him no part of his duties. And he was apprehensive that Prem might get his job.

So Prem stayed no longer than a week.

Here on the knoll the grass is just beginning to turn October yellow. The first clouds approaching winter cover the sky. The trees are very still. The birds are silent. Only a cricket keeps singing on the oak tree. Perhaps there will be a storm before evening. A storm like the one in which Prem arrived at the cottage with his wife and child—but that's jumping too far ahead...

After he had returned to his village, it was several months before I saw him again. His uncle told me he had taken up a job in Delhi. There was an address. It did not seem complete, but I resolved that when I was next in Delhi I would try to see him.

The opportunity came in May, as the hot winds of summer blew across the plains. It was the time of year when people who can afford it, try to get away to the hills. I dislike New Delhi at the best of times, and I hate it in summer. People compete with each other in being bad-tempered and mean. But I had to go down—I don't remember why, but it must have seemed very necessary at the time—and I took the opportunity to try and see Prem.

Nothing went right for me. Of course the address was all wrong, and I wandered about in a remote, dusty, treeless colony called Vasant Vihar (Spring Garden) for over two hours, asking all the domestic servants I came across if they could put me in touch with Prem Singh of Village Koli, Pauri Garhwal. There were innumerable Prem Singhs, but apparently none who belonged to Village Koli. I returned to my hotel and took two days to recover from heatstroke before returning to Mussoorie, thanking God for mountains!

And then the uncle gave notice. He'd found a better-paid job in Dehradun and was anxious to be off. I didn't try to stop him.

For the next six months I lived in the cottage without any help. I did not find this difficult. I was used to living alone. It wasn't service that I needed but companionship. In the cottage it was very quiet. The ghosts of long-dead residents were sympathetic but unobtrusive. The song of the whistling thrush was beautiful, but I knew he was not singing for me. Up the valley came the sound of a flute, but I never saw the flute player. My affinity was with the little red fox who roamed the hillside below the cottage. I met him one night and wrote these lines:

As I walked home last night
I saw a lone fox dancing
In the cold moonlight.
I stood and watched—then
Took the low road, knowing

the night was his by right.
Sometimes, when words ring true,
I'm like a lone fox dancing
In the morning dew.

During the rains, watching the dripping trees and the mist climbing the valley, I wrote a great deal of poetry. Loneliness is of value to poets. But poetry didn't bring me much money, and funds were low. And then, just as I was wondering if I would have to give up my freedom and take a job again, a publisher bought the paperback rights of one of my children's stories, and I was free to live and write as I pleased—for another three months!

That was in November. To celebrate, I took a long walk through the Landour bazaar and up the Tehri road. It was a good day for walking; and it was dark by the time I returned to the outskirts of the town. Someone stood waiting for me on the road above the cottage. I hurried past him.

If I am not for myself,
Who will be for me?
And if I am not for others,
What am I?
And if not now, when?

I startled myself with the memory of these words of Hillel, the ancient Hebrew sage. I walked back to the shadows where the youth stood, and saw that it was Prem.

'Prem!' I said. 'Why are you sitting out here, in the cold? Why did you not go to the house?'

'I went, sir, but there was a lock on the door. I thought you had gone away.'

'And you were going to remain here, on the road?'

'Only for tonight. I would have gone down to Dehra in the morning.'

'Come, let's go home. I have been waiting for you. I looked for you in Delhi, but could not find the place where you were working.'

'I have left them now.'

'And your uncle has left me. So will you work for me now?'

'For as long as you wish.'

'For as long as the gods wish.'

We did not go straight home, but returned to the bazaar and took our meal in the Sindhi Sweet Shop—hot puris and strong sweet tea.

We walked home together in the bright moonlight. I felt sorry for the little fox dancing alone.

That was twenty years ago, and Prem and his wife and three children are still with me. But we live in a different house now, on another hill.

On Fairy Hill

THOSE LITTLE GREEN LIGHTS THAT I USED TO SEE, TWINKLING away on Pari Tibba—there had to be a scientific explanation for them, I was sure. After dark we see or hear many things that seem mysterious, irrational. And then by the clear light of day we find that the magic, the mystery has an explanation after all.

But I did see those lights occasionally—late at night, when I walked home from town to my little cottage at the edge of the forest. They moved too fast for them to be torches or lanterns carried by people. And as there were no roads on Pari Tibba, they could not have been cycle or cart lamps. Someone told me there was phosphorus in the rocks, and that this probably accounted for the luminous glow emanating from the hillside late at night. Possibly; but I was not convinced.

My encounter with the little people happened by the light of day.

One morning, early in April, purely on an impulse, I decided to climb to the top of Pari Tibba and look around for myself. It was springtime in the Himalayan foothills. The sap was rising—in the trees, in the grass, in the wild flowers, in my own veins.

I took the path through the oak forest, down to the little steam at the bottom of the hill, and then up the steep slope of Pari Tibba, hill of the fairies.

It was quite a scramble getting to the top. The path ended at the stream. After that, I had to clutch at brambles and tufts of grass to make the ascent. Fallen pine needles, slippery underfoot, made it difficult to get a foothold. But finally I made it to the top—a grassy plateau fringed by pines and a few wild medlar trees now clothed in white blossom.

It was a pretty spot. And as I was hot and sweaty, I removed most of my clothing and lay down under a medlar to rest. The climb had been quite tiring. But a fresh breeze soon brought me back to life. It made a soft humming sound in the pines. And the grass, sprinkled with yellow buttercups, buzzed with the sound of crickets and grasshoppers.

After some time I stood up and surveyed the scene. To the north, Landour with its rusty red-roofed cottages; to the south, the wide valley and a silver stream flowing towards the Ganga. To the west, rolling hills, patches of forest, and a small village tucked into a fold of the mountain.

Disturbed by my presence, a barking deer ran across the clearing and down the opposite slope. A band of long-tailed blue magpies rose from the oak trees, glided across the knoll, and settled in another strand of oaks.

I was alone. Alone with the wind and the sky. It had probably been months, possibly years, since any human had passed that way. The soft lush grass looked most inviting. I lay down again on the sun-warmed sward. Pressed and bruised by my weight, catmint and clover gave out a soft fragrance. A ladybird climbed up my leg and began to explore my body. A swarm of white butterflies fluttered around me.

I slept.

I have no idea how long I slept, but when I awoke it was to experience an unusual, soothing sensation all over my limbs, as though they were being gently stroked with rose-petals.

All lethargy gone, I opened my eyes to find a little girl—or was it a woman?—about two inches high, sitting cross-legged on my chest and studying me intently. Her hair fell in long black tresses. Her skin was the colour of honey. Her firm little breasts were like tiny acorns. She held a buttercup, larger than her hand, and with it she was stroking my tingling flesh.

I was tingling all over. A sensation of sensual joy surged through my limbs.

A tiny boy—man?—completely naked, now joined the elfin girl, and they held hands and looked into my eyes, smiling, their teeth little pearls, their lips soft petals of apricot blossom. Were these the nature spirits, the flower fairies, I had often dreamt of? I raised my head and saw that there were scores of little people all over me—exploring my legs, thighs, waist and arms. Delicate, caring, gentle, caressing creatures. They wanted to love me!

Some of them were laving me with dew or pollen or some soft essence. I closed my eyes. Waves of pure physical pleasure swept over me. I had never known anything like it. My limbs turned to water. The sky revolved around me, and I must have fainted.

When I awoke, perhaps an hour later, the little people had gone. A fragrance of honeysuckle lingered in the air. A deep rumble overhead made me look up. Dark clouds had gathered, threatening rain. Had the thunder frightened them away, to their abode beneath the rocks and tree-roots? Or had they simply tired of sporting with a strange newcomer? Mischievous they were; for when I looked around for my clothes I could not find them anywhere.

A wave of panic surged over me. I ran here and there, looking behind shrubs and tree trunks, but to no avail. My clothes had disappeared, along with the fairies—if, indeed, they were fairies!

It began to rain. Large drops cannoned off the dry rocks. Then it hailed and soon the slope was covered with ice. There was no shelter. Naked, I ran down the path to the stream. There was no one to see me—only a wild mountain-goat, speeding away in the opposite direction. Gusts of wind slashed rain and hail across my face and body. Panting and shivering, I took shelter beneath an overhanging rock until the storm had passed. By then it was almost dusk and I was able to ascend the path to my cottage without encountering anyone, apart from a band of startled langoors, who chattered excitedly on seeing me.

I couldn't stop shivering, so I went straight to bed. I slept a deep, dreamless sleep and woke up the next morning with a high fever.

Mechanically I dressed, made myself some breakfast and tried to get through the morning's chores. When I took my temperature I found it was a hundred and four. So I swallowed a tablet and went back to bed.

There I lay until late afternoon, when the postman's knocking woke me. I left my letters unopened on my desk (that in itself was unusual) and returned to my bed.

The fever lasted almost a week and left me weak and half-starved. I couldn't have climbed Pari Tibba again, even if I'd wanted to; but I reclined on my window-seat and looked at the clouds drifting over that desolate hill. Desolate it seemed, and yet strangely inhabited. When it grew dark, I waited for those little green fairy lights to appear; but these, it seemed, were now to be denied to me.

And so I returned to my desk, my typewriter, my newspaper articles and correspondence. It was a lonely period in my life. My marriage hadn't worked out: my wife, fond of high society and averse to living with an unsuccessful writer in a remote cottage in the woods, was following her own, more successful career in Mumbai. I had always been rather half-hearted in my approach to making money, whereas she had always wanted more and more of it. She left me—left me with my books and my dreams....

Had it all been a dream, that strange episode on Pari Tibba? Had an overactive imagination conjured up those aerial spirits, those Siddhas of the Upper Air? Or were they underground people, living deep within the bowels of the hill? If I was going to keep my sanity I knew I had better get on with the more mundane aspects of living—such as going into town to buy my groceries, mending the leaking roof, paying the electricity bill, plodding up to the post office, and remembering to deposit the odd cheque that came my way. All the mundane things that made life so dull and dreary.

The truth is, what we commonly call life is not life at all. Its routine and settled ways are the curse of life, and we will do almost anything to get away from the trivial, even if it is only for a few hours of forgetfulness in alcohol, drugs, forbidden sex, or golf. Some of us would even go underground with the fairies, those little people who have sought refuge in Mother Earth from mankind's killing ways; for they are as vulnerable as butterflies and flowers. All things beautiful are easily destroyed.

I am sitting at my window in the gathering dark, penning these stray thoughts, when I see them coming—hand in hand, walking on a swirl of mist, radiant, suffused with all the colours of the rainbow. For a rainbow has formed a bridge from them, from Pari Tibba, to the edge of my window.

I am ready to go, to love and be loved, in their secret lairs or in the upper air—far from the stifling confines of the world in which we toil....

Come, fairies, carry me away, to love me as you did that summer's day!

The Playing Fields of Simla

IT HAD BEEN A LONELY WINTER FOR A TWELVE-YEAR-OLD BOY. I hadn't really got over my father's untimely death two years previously; nor had I as yet reconciled myself to my mother's marriage to the Punjabi gentleman who dealt in second-hand cars. The three-month winter break over, I was almost happy to return to my boarding school in Simla—that elegant hill station once celebrated by Kipling and soon to lose its status as the summer capital of the Raj in India.

It wasn't as though I had many friends at school. I had always been a bit of a loner, shy and reserved, looking out only for my father's rare visits—on his brief leaves from RAF duties—and to my sharing his tent or air-force hutment outside Delhi or Karachi. Those unsettled but happy days would not come again. I needed a friend but it was not easy to find one among a horde of rowdy, pea-shooting fourth formers, who carved their names on desks and stuck chewing gum on the class teacher's chair. Had I grown up with other children, I might have developed a taste for schoolboy anarchy; but, in sharing my father's loneliness after his separation from my mother, I had turned into a premature adult. The mixed nature of my reading—Dickens, Richmal Crompton, Tagore and *Champion* and *Film Fun* comics—probably reflected the confused state of my life. A book reader was rare even in those pre-electronic times. On rainy days most boys played cards or Monopoly, or listened to Artie Shaw on the wind-up gramophone in the common room.

After a month in the fourth form I began to notice a new boy, Omar, and then only because he was a quiet, almost taciturn person who took no part in the form's feverish attempts to imitate the Marx Brothers at the circus. He showed no resentment at the prevailing anarchy, nor did he make a move to participate in it. Once he caught me looking at him, and he smiled ruefully, tolerantly. Did I sense another adult in the class? Someone who was a little older than his years?

Even before we began talking to each other, Omar and I developed an understanding of sorts, and we'd nod almost respectfully to each other when we met in the classroom corridors or the environs of dining hall or dormitory. We were not in the same house. The house system practised its own form of apartheid, whereby a member of, say, Curzon House was not expected to fraternize with someone belonging to Rivaz or Lefroy! Those public schools certainly knew how to clamp you into compartments. However, these barriers vanished when Omar and I found ourselves selected for the School Colts' hockey team—Omar as a fullback, I as goalkeeper. I think a defensive position suited me by nature. In all modesty I have to say that I made a good goalkeeper, both at hockey and football. And fifty years on, I am still keeping goal. Then I did it between goalposts, now I do it off the field—protecting a family, protecting my independence as a writer...

The taciturn Omar now spoke to me occasionally, and we combined well on the field of play. A good understanding is needed between goalkeeper and fullback. We were on the same wavelength. I anticipated his moves, he was familiar with mine. Years later, when I read Conrad's *The Secret Sharer,* I thought of Omar.

It wasn't until we were away from the confines of school, classroom and dining hall that our friendship flourished. The hockey team travelled to Sanawar on the next mountain range, where we were to play a couple of matches against our old rivals, the Lawrence Royal Military School. This had been my father's old school, but I did not know that in his time it had also been a military orphanage. Grandfather, who had been a private foot soldier—of the likes of Kipling's Mulvaney, Otheris and Learoyd—had joined the Scottish Rifles after leaving home at the age of seventeen. He had died while his children were still very young, but my father's more rounded education had enabled him to become an officer.

Omar and I were thrown together a good deal during the visit to Sanawar, and in our more leisurely moments, strolling undisturbed around a school where we were guests and not pupils, we exchanged life histories and other confidences. Omar, too, had lost his father—had I sensed that before?—shot in some tribal encounter on the Frontier, for he hailed from the lawless lands beyond Peshawar. A wealthy uncle was seeing to Omar's education. The RAF was now seeing to mine.

We wandered into the school chapel, and there I found my father's name—A.A. Bond—on the school's roll of honour board: old boys who had lost their lives while serving during the two World Wars.

'What did his initials stand for?' asked Omar.

'Aubrey Alexander.'

'Unusual names, like yours. Why did your parents call you Ruskin?'

'I am not sure. I think my father liked the works of John Ruskin, who wrote on serious subjects like art and architecture. I don't think anyone reads him now. They'll read me, though!' I had already started writing my first book. It was called *Nine Months* (the length of the school term, not a pregnancy), and it described some of the happenings at school and lampooned a few of our teachers. I had filled three slim exercise books with this premature literary project, and I allowed Omar to go through them. He must have been my first reader and critic. 'They're very interesting,' he said, 'but you'll get into trouble if someone finds them. Especially Mr Oliver.' And he read out an offending verse:

> Olly, Olly, Olly, with his balls on a trolley,
> And his arse all painted green!

I have to admit it wasn't great literature. I was better at hockey and football. I made some spectacular saves, and we won our matches against Sanawar. When we returned to Simla, we were school heroes for a couple of days and lost some of our reticence; we were even a little more forthcoming with other boys. And then Mr Fisher, my housemaster, discovered my literary opus, *Nine Months,* under my mattress, and took it away and read it (as he told me later) from cover to cover. Corporal punishment then being in vogue, I was given six of the best with a springy malacca cane, and my manuscript was torn up and deposited in Fisher's wastepaper basket. All I had to show for my efforts were some purple welts on my bottom. These were proudly displayed to all who were interested, and

I was a hero for another two days.

'Will you go away too when the British leave India?' Omar asked me one day.

'I don't think so,' I said. 'My stepfather is Indian.'

'Everyone is saying that our leaders and the British are going to divide the country. Simla will be in India, Peshawar in Pakistan!'

'Oh, it won't happen,' I said glibly. 'How can they cut up such a big country?' But even as we chatted about the possibility, Nehru and Jinnah and Mountbatten and all those who mattered were preparing their instruments for major surgery.

Before their decision impinged on our lives and everyone else's, we found a little freedom of our own—in an underground tunnel that we discovered below the third flat.

It was really part of an old, disused drainage system, and when Omar and I began exploring it, we had no idea just how far it extended. After crawling along on our bellies for some twenty feet, we found ourselves in complete darkness. Omar had brought along a small pencil torch, and with its help we continued writhing forward (moving backwards would have been quite impossible) until we saw a glimmer of light at the end of the tunnel. Dusty, musty, very scruffy, we emerged at last on to a grassy knoll, a little way outside the school boundary.

It's always a great thrill to escape beyond the boundaries that adults have devised. Here we were in unknown territory. To travel without passports—that would be the ultimate in freedom!

But more passports were on their way and more boundaries.

Lord Mountbatten, viceroy and governor-general-to-be, came for our Founder's Day and gave away the prizes. I had won a prize for something or the other, and mounted the rostrum to receive my book from this towering, handsome man in his pinstriped suit. Bishop Cotton's was then the premier school of India, often referred to as the 'Eton of the East'. Viceroys and governors had graced its functions. Many of its boys had gone on to eminence in the civil services and armed forces. There was one 'old boy' about whom they maintained a stolid silence—General Dyer, who had ordered the massacre at Amritsar and destroyed the trust that had been building up between Britain and India.

Now Mountbatten spoke of the momentous events that were happening all around us—the War had just come to an end, the United Nations held out the promise of a world living in peace and harmony, and India, an equal partner with Britain, would be among the great nations...

A few weeks later, Bengal and Punjab provinces were bisected. Riots flared up across northern India, and there was a great exodus of people crossing the newly drawn frontiers of Pakistan and India. Homes were destroyed, thousands lost their lives.

The common-room radio and the occasional newspaper kept us abreast of events, but in our tunnel, Omar and I felt immune from all that was happening, worlds away from all the pillage, murder and revenge. And outside the tunnel, on the pine knoll below the school, there was fresh untrodden grass, sprinkled with clover and daisies, the only sounds the hammering of a woodpecker, the distant insistent call of the Himalayan barbet. Who could touch us there?

'And when all the wars are done,' I said, 'a butterfly will still be beautiful.'

'Did you read that somewhere?'

'No, it just came into my head.'

'Already you're a writer.'

'No, I want to play hockey for India or football for Arsenal.

Only winning teams!'

'You can't win forever. Better to be a writer.'

When the monsoon rains arrived, the tunnel was flooded, the drain choked with rubble. We were allowed out to the cinema to see Lawrence Olivier's *Hamlet*, a film that did nothing to raise our spirits on a wet and gloomy afternoon—but it was our last picture that year, because communal riots suddenly broke out in Simla's Lower Bazaar, an area that was still much as Kipling had described it—'a man who knows his way there can defy all the police of India's summer capital'—and we were confined to school indefinitely.

One morning after chapel, the headmaster announced that the Muslim boys—those who had their homes in what was now Pakistan—would have to be evacuated, sent to their homes across the border with an armed convoy.

The tunnel no longer provided an escape for us. The bazaar was out of bounds. The flooded playing field was deserted. Omar and I sat on a damp wooden bench and talked about the future in vaguely hopeful terms; but we didn't solve any problems. Mountbatten and Nehru and Jinnah were doing all the solving.

It was soon time for Omar to leave—he along with some fifty other boys from Lahore, Pindi and Peshawar. The rest of us—Hindus, Christians, Parsis—helped them load their luggage into the waiting trucks. A couple of boys broke down and wept. So did our departing school captain, a Pathan who had been known for his stoic and unemotional demeanour. Omar waved cheerfully to me and I waved back. We had vowed to meet again some day.

The convoy got through safely enough. There was only one casualty—the school cook, who had strayed into an off-limits area in the foothill town of Kalka and been set upon by a mob.

He wasn't seen again.

Towards the end of the school year, just as we were all getting ready to leave for the school holidays, I received a letter from Omar. He told me something about his new school and how he missed my company and our games and our tunnel to freedom. I replied and gave him my home address, but I did not hear from him again. The land, though divided, was still a big one, and we were very small.

Some seventeen or eighteen years later I did get news of Omar, but in an entirely different context. India and Pakistan were at war and in a bombing raid over Ambala, not far from Simla, a Pakistani plane was shot down. Its crew died in the crash. One of them, I learnt later, was Omar.

Did he, I wonder, get a glimpse of the playing fields we knew so well as boys?

Perhaps memories of his schooldays flooded back as he flew over the foothills. Perhaps he remembered the tunnel through which we were able to make our little escape to freedom.

But there are no tunnels in the sky.

Gone Fishing

THE HOUSE WAS CALLED 'UNDERCLIFF', BECAUSE THAT'S WHERE it stood—under a cliff. The man who went away—the owner of the house—was Robert Astley. And the man who stayed behind—the old family retainer—was Prem Bahadur.

Astley had been gone many years. He was still a bachelor in his late thirties when he'd suddenly decided that he wanted adventure, romance, faraway places; and he'd given the keys of the house to Prem Bahadur—who'd served the family for thirty years—and had set off on his travels.

Someone saw him in Sri Lanka. He'd been heard of in Burma, around the ruby mines at Mogok. Then he turned up in Java, seeking a passage through the Sunda Straits. After that the trail petered out. Years passed. The house in the hill-station remained empty.

But Prem Bahadur was still there, living in an outhouse.

Every day he opened up Undercliff, dusted the furniture in all the rooms, made sure that the bedsheets and pillowcases were clean, and set out Astley's dressing-gown and slippers.

In the old days, whenever Astley had come home after a

journey or a long tramp in the hills, he had liked to bathe and change into his gown and slippers, no matter what the hour. Prem Bahadur still kept them ready. He was convinced that Robert would return one day.

Astley himself had said so.

'Keep everything ready for me, Prem, old chap. I may be back after a year, or two years, or even longer, but I'll be back, I promise you. On the first of every month I want you to go to my lawyer, Mr Kapoor. He'll give you your salary and any money that's needed for the rates and repairs. I want you to keep the house tip-top!'

'Will you bring back a wife, Sahib?'

'Lord, no! Whatever put that idea in your head?'

'I thought, perhaps—because you wanted the house kept ready….'

'Ready for me, Prem. I don't want to come home and find the old place falling down.'

And so Prem had taken care of the house—although there was no news from Astley. What had happened to him? The mystery provided a talking-point whenever local people met on the Mall. And in the bazaar the shopkeepers missed Astley because he was a man who spent freely.

His relatives still believed him to be alive. Only a few months back a brother had turned up—a brother who had a farm in Canada and could not stay in India for long. He had deposited a further sum with the lawyer and told Prem to carry on as before. The salary provided Prem with his few needs. Moreover, he was convinced that Robert would return.

Another man might have neglected the house and grounds, but not Prem Bahadur. He had a genuine regard for the absent owner. Prem was much older—now almost sixty and none too strong, suffering from pleurisy and other chest troubles—but he remembered Robert as both a boy and a young man. They had been together on numerous hunting and fishing trips in the mountains. They had slept out under the stars, bathed in icy mountain streams, and eaten from the same cooking-pot. Once, when crossing a small river, they had been swept downstream by a flash-flood, a wall of water that came thundering down the gorges without any warning during the rainy season. Together they had struggled back to safety. Back in the hill-station, Astley told everyone that Prem had saved his life; while Prem was equally insistent that he owed his life to Robert.

This year the monsoon had begun early and ended late. It dragged on through most of September, and Prem Bahadur's cough grew worse and his breathing more difficult.

He lay on his charpai on the veranda, staring out at the garden, which was beginning to get out of hand, a tangle of dahlias, snake-lilies and convolvulus. The sun finally came out. The wind shifted from the southwest to the northwest, and swept the clouds away.

Prem Bahadur had taken his charpai into the garden, and was lying in the sun, puffing at his small hookah, when he saw Robert Astley at the gate.

He tried to get up but his legs would not oblige him. The hookah slipped from his hand.

Astley came walking down the garden path and stopped in front of the old retainer, smiling down at him. He did not look a day older than when Prem Bahadur had last seen him.

'So you have come at last,' said Prem.

'I told you I'd return.'

'It has been many years. But you have not changed.'

'Nor have you, old chap.'

'I have grown old and sick and feeble.'

'You'll be fine now. That's why I've come.'

'I'll open the house,' said Prem, and this time he found himself getting up quite easily.

'It isn't necessary,' said Astley.

'But all is ready for you!'

'I know. I have heard of how well you have looked after everything. Come then, let's take a last look round. We cannot stay, you know.'

Prem was a little mystified but he opened the front door and took Robert through the drawing-room and up the stairs to the bedroom. Robert saw the dressing-gown and the slippers, and he placed his hand gently on the old man's shoulder.

When they returned downstairs and emerged into the sunlight, Prem was surprised to see himself—or rather his skinny body—stretched out on the charpai. The hookah lay on the ground, where it had fallen.

Prem looked at Astley in bewilderment.

'But who is that—lying there?'

'It was you. Only the husk now, the empty shell. This is the real you, standing here beside me.'

'You came for me?'

'I couldn't come until you were ready. As for me, I left *my* shell a long time ago. But you were determined to hang on, keeping this house together. Are you ready now?'

'And the house?'

'Others will live in it. Nothing is lost for ever, everything begins again. ... But come, it's time to go fishing....'

Astley took Prem by the arm, and they walked through the dappled sunlight under the deodars and finally left that place for another.

Binya Passes By

WHILE I WAS WALKING HOME ONE DAY, ALONG THE PATH through the pines, I heard a girl singing.

It was summer in the hills, and the trees were in new leaf. The walnuts and cherries were just beginning to form between the leaves.

The wind was still and the trees were hushed, and the song came to me clearly; but it was not the words—which I could not follow—or the rise and fall of the melody which held me in thrall, but the voice itself, which was a young and tender voice.

I left the path and scrambled down the slope, slipping on fallen pine needles. But when I came to the bottom of the slope, the singing had stopped and no one was there. 'I'm sure I heard someone singing,' I said to myself; but I may have been wrong. In the hills it is always possible to be wrong.

So I walked on home, and presently I heard another song, but this time it was the whistling thrush rendering a broken melody, singing of dark, sweet secrets in the depths of the forest.

I had little to sing about myself, as the electricity bill hadn't been paid, and there was nothing in the bank, and my second novel had just been turned down by another publisher. Still, it was summer, and men and animals were drowsy, and so too were my creditors. The distant mountains loomed purple in the shimmering dust-haze.

I walked through the pines again, but I did not hear the singing. And then for a week I did not leave the cottage, as the novel had to be rewritten, and I worked hard at it, pausing only to eat and sleep and take note of the leaves turning a darker green.

The window opened on to the forest. Trees reached up to the window. Oak, maple, walnut. Higher up the hill, the pines started, and further on, armies of deodars marched over the mountains. And the mountains rose higher, and the trees grew stunted until they finally disappeared and only the black spirit-haunted rocks rose up to meet the everlasting snows. Those peaks cradled the sky. I could not see them from my windows. But on clear mornings they could be seen from the pass on the Tehri road.

There was a stream at the bottom of the hill. One morning, quite early, I went down to the stream, and using the boulders as stepping stones, moved downstream for about half a mile. Then I lay down to rest on a flat rock, in the shade of a wild cherry tree, and watched the sun shifting through the branches as it rose over the hill called Pari Tibba (Fairy Hill) and slid down the steep slope into the valley. The air was very still and already the birds were silent. The only sound came from the water running over the stony bed of the stream. I had lain there ten, perhaps fifteen, minutes when I began to feel that someone was watching me.

Someone in the trees, in the shadows, still and watchful. Nothing moved; not a stone shifted, not a twig broke; but someone was watching me. I felt terribly exposed; not to danger, but to the scrutiny of unknown eyes. So I left the rock and, finding a path through the trees, began climbing the hill again.

It was warm work. The sun was up, and there was no breeze. I was perspiring profusely by the time I got to the top of the hill. There was no sign of my unseen watcher. Two lean cows grazed on the short grass; the tinkling of their bells was the only sound in the sultry summer air.

That song again! The same song, the same singer. I heard her from my window. And putting aside the book I was reading, I leant out of the window and started down through the trees. But the foliage was too heavy, and the singer too far away for me to be able to make her out. 'Should I go and look for her?' I wondered. Or is it better this way—heard but not seen? For having fallen in love with a song, must it follow that I will fall in love with the singer? No. But surely it is the voice, and not the song that has touched me... Presently the singing ended, and I turned away from the window.

◆

A girl was gathering bilberries on the hillside. She was fresh-faced, honey-coloured; her lips were stained with purple juice. She smiled at me. 'Are they good to eat?' I asked.

She opened her fist and thrust out her hand, which was full of berries, bruised and crushed. I took one and put it in my mouth. It had a sharp, sour taste. 'It is good,' I said. Finding that I could speak haltingly in her language, she came nearer, said, 'Take more then,' and filled my hand with bilberries. Her fingers touched mine. The sensation was almost unique; for it was nine or ten years since my hand had touched a girl's.

'Where do you live?' I asked. She pointed across the valley to where a small village straddled the slopes of a terraced hill.

'It's quite far,' I said. 'Do you always come so far from home?'

'I go further than this,' she said. 'The cows must find fresh grass. And there is wood to gather and grass to cut.' She showed me the sickle held by the cloth tied firmly about her waist. 'Sometimes I go to the top of Pari Tibba, sometimes to the valley beyond. Have you been there?'

'No. But I will go some day.'

'It is always windy on Pari Tibba.'

'Is it true that there are fairies there?'

She laughed. 'That is what people say. But those are people who have never been there. I do not see fairies on Pari Tibba. It is said that there are ghosts in the ruins on the hill. But I do not see any ghosts.'

'I have heard of the ghosts,' I said. 'Two lovers who ran away and took shelter in a ruined cottage. At night there was a storm, and they were killed by lightning. Is it true, this story?'

'It happened many years ago, before I was born. I have heard the story. But there are no ghosts on Pari Tibba.'

'How old are you?' I asked.

'Fifteen, sixteen, I do not know for sure.'

'Doesn't your mother know?'

'She is dead. And my grandmother has forgotten. And my brother, he is younger than me and he's forgotten his own age. Is it important to remember?'

'No, it is not important. Not here, anyway. Not in the hills. To a mountain, a hundred years are but as a day.'

'Are you very old?' she asked.

'I hope not. Do I look very old?'

'Only a hundred,' she said, and laughed, and the silver

bangles on her wrists tinkled as she put her hand up to her laughing face.

'Why do you laugh?' I asked.

'Because you looked as though you believed me. How old are you?'

'Thirty-five, thirty-six, I do not remember.'

'Ah, it is better to forget!'

'That's true,' I said, 'but sometimes one has to fill in forms and things like that, and then one has to state one's age.'

'I have never filled a form. I have never seen one.'

'And I hope you never will. It is a piece of paper covered with useless information. It is all a part of human progress.'

'Progress?'

'Yes. Are you unhappy?'

'No.'

'Do you go hungry?'

'No.'

'Then you don't need progress. Wild bilberries are better.'

She went away without saying goodbye. The cows had strayed and she ran after them, calling them by name: 'Neelu, Neelu!' (Blue) and 'Bhuri!' (Old One). Her bare feet moved swiftly over the rocks and dry grass.

◆

Early May. The cicadas were singing in the forests; or rather, orchestrating, since they make the sound with their legs. The whistling thrushes pursued each other over the treetops, in acrobatic love-flights. Sometimes the langoors visited the oak trees, to feed on the leaves. As I moved down the path to the stream, I heard the same singing; and coming suddenly upon the clearing near the water's edge, I saw the girl sitting on a rock, her feet in the rushing water—the same girl who had given me bilberries. Strangely enough, I had not guessed that she was the singer. Unseen voices conjure up fanciful images. I had imagined a woodland nymph, a graceful, delicate, beautiful, goddess-like creature; not a mischievous-eyed, round-faced, juice-stained, slightly ragged pixie. Her dhoti—a rough, homespun sari—faded and torn; an impractical garment, I thought, for running about on the hillside, but the village folk put their girls into dhotis before they are twelve. She'd compromised by hitching it up, and by strengthening the waist with a length of cloth bound tightly about her, but she'd have been more at ease in the long, flounced skirt worn in the further hills.

But I was not disillusioned. I had clearly taken a fancy to her cherubic, open countenance; and the sweetness of her voice added to her charms.

I watched her from the banks of the stream, and presently she looked up, grinned, and stuck her tongue out at me.

'That's a nice way to greet me,' I said. 'Have I offended you?'

'You surprised me. Why did you not call out?'

'Because I was listening to your singing. I did not wish to speak until you had finished.'

'It was only a song.'

'But you sang it sweetly.'

She smiled. 'Have you brought anything to eat?'

'No. Are you hungry?'

'At this time I get hungry. When you come to meet me you must always bring something to eat.'

'But I didn't come to meet you. I didn't know you would be here.'

'You do not wish to meet me?'

'I didn't mean that. It is nice to meet you.'

'You will meet me if you keep coming into the forest. So always bring something to eat.'

'I will do so next time. Shall I pick you some berries?'

'You will have to go to the top of the hill again to find the Kingora bushes.'

'I don't mind. If you are hungry, I will bring some.'

'All right,' she said, and looked down at her feet, which were still in the water.

Like some knight-errant of old, I toiled up the hill again until I found the bilberry bushes; and stuffing my pockets with berries, I returned to the stream. But when I got there I found she'd slipped away. The cowbells tinkled on the far hill.

◆

Glow-worms shone fitfully in the dark. The night was full of sounds—the *tonk-tonk* of a nightjar, the cry of a barking deer, the shuffling of porcupines, the soft flip-flop of moths beating against the windowpanes. On the hill across the valley, lights flickered in the small village—the dim lights of kerosene lamps swinging in the dark.

'What is your name?' I asked, when we met again on the path through the pine forest.

'Binya,' she said. 'What is yours?'

'I've no name.'

'All right, Mr No-name.'

'I mean, I haven't made a name for myself. We must make our own names, don't you think?'

'Binya is my name. I do not wish to have any other. Where are you going?'

'Nowhere.'

'No-name goes nowhere! Then you cannot come with me, because I am going home and my grandmother will set the village dogs on you if you follow me.' And laughing, she ran down the path to the stream; she knew I could not catch up with her.

◆

Her face streamed summer rain as she climbed the steep hill, calling the white cow home. She seemed very tiny on the windswept mountainside; a twist of hair lay flat against her forehead, and her torn blue dhoti clung to her firm round thighs. I went to her with an umbrella to give her shelter. She stood with me beneath the umbrella and let me put my arm around her. Then she turned her face up to mine, wonderingly, and I kissed her quickly, softly on the lips. Her lips tasted of raindrops and mint. And then she left me there, so gallant in the blistering rain. She ran home laughing. But it was worth the drenching.

Another day I heard her calling to me—'No-name, Mister No-name!'—but I couldn't see her, and it was some time before I found her, halfway up a cherry tree, her feet pressed firmly against the bark, her dhoti tucked up between her thighs—fair, rounded thighs, and legs that were strong and vigorous.

'The cherries are not ripe,' I said.

'They are never ripe. But I like them green and sour. Will you come into the tree?'

'If I can still climb a tree,' I said.

'My grandmother is over sixty, and *she* can climb trees.'

'Well, I wouldn't mind being more adventurous at sixty. There's not so much to lose then.' I climbed into the tree without much difficulty, but I did not think the higher branches would take my weight; so I remained standing in the fork of the tree, my face on a level with Binya's breasts. I put my hand against her waist, and kissed her on the soft inside of her arm. She did not say anything. But she took me by the hand and helped me to climb a little higher, and I put my arm around her, as much to support myself as to be close to her.

◆

The full moon rides high, shining through the tall oak trees near the window. The night is full of sounds, crickets, the *tonk-tonk* of a nightjar, and floating across the valley from your village, the sound of drums beating, and people singing. It is a festival day, and there will be feasting in your home. Are you singing too, tonight? And are you thinking of me, as you sing, as you laugh, as you dance with your friends? I am sitting here alone, and so I have no one to think of but you.

Binya…I take your name again and again—as though by taking it, I can make you hear me, come to me, walking over the moonlit mountain….

There are spirits abroad tonight. They move silently in the trees; they hover about the window at which I sit; they take up with the wind and rush about the house. Spirits of the trees, spirits of the old house. An old lady died here last year. She'd lived in the house for over thirty years; something of her personality surely dwells here still. When I look into the tall, old mirror which was hers, I sometimes catch a glimpse of her pale face and long, golden hair. She likes me, I think, and the house is kind to me. Would she be jealous of you, Binya?

The music and singing grows louder. I can imagine your face glowing in the firelight. Your eyes shine with laughter. You have all those people near you and I have only the stars, and the nightjar, and the ghost in the mirror.

◆

I woke early, while the dew was still fresh on the grass, and walked down the hill to the stream, and then up to a little knoll where a pine tree grew in solitary splendour, the wind going *hoo-hoo* in its slender branches. This was my favourite place, my place of power, where I came to renew myself from time to time. I lay on the grass, dreaming. The sky in its blueness swung round above me. An eagle soared in the distance. I heard her voice down among the trees; or I thought I heard it. But when I went to look, I could not find her.

I'd always prided myself on my rationality; had taught myself to be wary of emotional states, like 'falling in love', which turned out to be ephemeral and illusory. And although I told myself again and again that the attraction was purely physical, on my part as well as hers, I had to admit to myself that my feelings towards Binya differed from the feelings I'd had for others; and that while sex had often been for me a celebration, it had, like any other feast, resulted in satiety, a need for change, a desire to forget....

Binya represented something else—something wild, dreamlike, fairy-like. She moved close to the spirit-haunted rocks, the old trees, the young grass; she had absorbed something from them—a primeval innocence, an unconcern with the passing of time and events, an affinity with the forest and the mountains; this made her special and magical.

And so, when three, four, five days went by, and I did not find her on the hillside, I went through all the pangs of frustrated love: had she forgotten me and gone elsewhere? Had we been seen together, and was she being kept at home? Was she ill? Or, had she been spirited away?

I could hardly go and ask for her. I would probably be driven from the village. It straddled the opposite hill, a cluster of slate-roof houses, a pattern of little terraced fields. I could see figures in the fields, but they were too far away, too tiny for me to be able to recognize anyone. She had gone to her mother's village a hundred miles away, or so a small boy told me.

And so I brooded; walked disconsolately through the oak forest hardly listening to the birds—the sweet-throated whistling thrush; the shrill barbet; the mellow-voiced doves. Happiness had always made me more responsive to nature. Feeling miserable, my thoughts turned inward. I brooded upon the trickery of time and circumstance; I felt the years were passing by, *had* passed by, like waves on a receding tide, leaving me washed up like a bit of flotsam on a lonely beach. But at the same time, the whistling thrush seemed to mock at me, calling tantalizingly from the shadows of the ravine; 'It isn't time that's passing by, it is you and I, it is you and I....'

Then I forced myself to snap out of my melancholy. I kept away from the hillside and the forest. I did not look towards the village. I buried myself in my work, tried to think objectively, and wrote an article on 'The inscriptions on the iron pillar at Kalsi'; very learned, very dry, very sensible.

But at night I was assailed by the thoughts of Binya. I could not sleep. I switched on the light, and there she was, smiling at me from the looking glass, replacing the image of the old lady who had watched over me for so long.

The Cherry Tree

ONE DAY, WHEN RAKESH WAS SIX, HE WALKED HOME FROM THE Mussoorie bazaar eating cherries. They were a little sweet, a little sour; small, bright red cherries which had come all the way from the Kashmir Valley.

Here in the Himalayan foothills where Rakesh lived, there were not many fruit trees. The soil was stony, and the dry cold winds stunted the growth of most plants. But on the more sheltered slopes there were forests of oak and deodar.

Rakesh lived with his grandfather on the outskirts of Mussoorie, just where the forest began. His father and mother lived in a small village fifty miles away, where they grew maize and rice and barley in narrow terraced fields on the lower slopes of the mountain. But there were no schools in the village, and Rakesh's parents were keen that he should go to school. As soon as he was of schoolgoing age, they sent him to stay with his grandfather in Mussoorie.

Grandfather was a retired forest ranger. He had a little cottage outside the town.

Rakesh was on his way home from school when he bought

the cherries. He paid fifty paise for the bunch. It took him about half an hour to walk home, and by the time he reached the cottage there were only three cherries left.

'Have a cherry, Grandfather,' he said, as soon as he saw his grandfather in the garden.

Grandfather took one cherry and Rakesh promptly ate the other two. He kept the last seed in his mouth for some time, rolling it round and round on his tongue until all the tang had gone. Then he placed the seed on the palm of his hand and studied it.

'Are cherry seeds lucky?' asked Rakesh.

'Of course.'

'Then I'll keep it.'

'Nothing is lucky if you put it away. If you want luck, you must put it to some use.'

'What can I do with a seed?'

'Plant it.'

So Rakesh found a small spade and began to dig up a flower bed.

'Hey, not there,' said Grandfather. 'I've sown mustard in that bed. Plant it in that shady corner where it won't be disturbed.'

Rakesh went to a corner of the garden where the earth was soft and yielding. He did not have to dig. He pressed the seed into the soil with his thumb and it went right in.

Then he had his lunch and ran off to play cricket with his friends and forgot all about the cherry seed.

When it was winter in the hills, a cold wind blew down from the snows and went *whoo-whoo-whoo* through the deodar trees, and the garden was dry and bare. In the evenings Grandfather told Rakesh stories—stories about people who turned into animals, and ghosts who lived in trees, and beans that jumped and stones that wept—and in turn Rakesh would read to him from the newspaper, Grandfather's eyesight being rather weak. Rakesh found the newspaper very dull—especially after the stories—but Grandfather wanted all the news...

They knew it was spring when the wild duck flew north again, to Siberia. Early in the morning, when he got up to chop wood and light a fire, Rakesh saw the V-shaped formation streaming northwards, the calls of the birds carrying clearly through the thin mountain air.

One morning in the garden, he bent to pick up what he thought was a small twig and found to his surprise that it was well rooted. He stared at it for a moment, then ran to fetch Grandfather, calling, 'Dada, come and look, the cherry tree has come up!'

'What cherry tree?' asked Grandfather, who had forgotten about it.

'The seed we planted last year—look, it's come up!'

Rakesh went down on his haunches, while Grandfather bent almost double and peered down at the tiny tree. It was about four inches high.

'Yes, it's a cherry tree,' said Grandfather. 'You should water it now and then.'

Rakesh ran indoors and came back with a bucket of water.

'Don't drown it!' said Grandfather.

Rakesh gave it a sprinkling and circled it with pebbles.

'What are the pebbles for?' asked Grandfather.

'For privacy,' said Rakesh.

He looked at the tree every morning but it did not seem to be growing very fast. So he stopped looking at it—except quickly, out of the corner of his eye. And, after a week or two, when he allowed himself to look at it properly, he found that it had grown—at least an inch!

That year the monsoon rains came early and Rakesh plodded to and from school in raincoat and gumboots. Ferns sprang from the trunks of trees, strange-looking lilies came up in the long grass, and even when it wasn't raining the trees dripped, and mist came curling up the valley. The cherry tree grew quickly in this season.

It was about two feet high when a goat entered the garden and ate all the leaves. Only the main stem and two thin branches remained.

'Never mind,' said Grandfather, seeing that Rakesh was upset. 'It will grow again, cherry trees are tough.'

Towards the end of the rainy season new leaves appeared on the tree. Then a woman cutting grass scrambled down the hillside, her scythe swishing through the heavy monsoon foliage. She did not try to avoid the tree: one sweep, and the cherry tree was cut in two.

When Grandfather saw what had happened, he went after the woman and scolded her; but the damage could not be repaired.

'Maybe it will die now,' said Rakesh.

'Maybe,' said Grandfather.

But the cherry tree had no intention of dying.

By the time summer came round again, it had sent out several new shoots with tender green leaves. Rakesh had grown taller too. He was eight now, a sturdy boy with curly black hair and deep black eyes. Blackberry eyes, Grandfather called them.

That monsoon Rakesh went home to his village, to help his father and mother with the planting and ploughing and sowing. He was thinner but stronger when he came back to Grandfather's house at the end of the rains, to find that the cherry tree had grown another foot. It was now up to his chest.

Even when there was rain, Rakesh would sometimes water the tree. He wanted it to know that he was there.

One day he found a bright green praying mantis perched on a branch, peering at him with bulging eyes. Rakesh let it remain there. It was the cherry tree's first visitor.

The next visitor was a hairy caterpillar, who started making a meal of the leaves. Rakesh removed it quickly and dropped it on a heap of dry leaves.

'They're pretty leaves,' said Rakesh. 'And they are always ready to dance. If there's a breeze.'

After Grandfather had come indoors, Rakesh went into the garden and lay down on the grass beneath the tree. He gazed up through the leaves at the great blue sky; and turning on his side, he could see the mountain striding away into the clouds. He was still lying beneath the tree when the evening shadows crept across the garden. Grandfather came back and sat down beside Rakesh, and they waited in silence until the stars came out and the nightjar began to call. In the forest below, the crickets and cicadas began tuning up; and suddenly the tree was full of the sounds of insects.

'There are so many trees in the forest,' said Rakesh. 'What's so special about this tree? Why do we like it so much?'

'We planted it ourselves,' said Grandfather. 'That's why it's special.'

'Just one small seed,' said Rakesh, and he touched the smooth bark of the tree that had grown. He ran his hand along the trunk of the tree and put his finger to the tip of a leaf. 'I wonder,' he whispered, 'is this what it feels to be God?'

Once upon a Mountain Time

My solitude is not my own, for I see now how much it belongs to them—and that I have a responsibility for it in their regard, not just in my own. It is because I am one with them that I owe it to them to be alone, and when I am alone they are not 'they' but my own self. There are no strangers!

—Thomas Merton, *Confessions of a Guilty Bystander*

THE TREES STAND WATCH OVER MY DAY-TO-DAY LIFE. THEY ARE the guardians of my conscience. I have no one else to answer to, so I live and work under the generous but highly principled supervision of the trees—especially the deodars, who stand on guard, unbending, on the slope above the cottage. The oak and maples are a little more tolerant, they have had to put up with a great deal, their branches continually lopped for fuel and fodder. 'What would *they* think?' I ask myself on many an occasion. 'What would they like me to do?' And I do what *I* think they would approve of most!

Well, it's nice to have someone to turn to...

The leaves are a fresh pale green in the spring rain. I can

look at the trees from my window—look down on them almost, because the window is on the first floor of the cottage, and the hillside runs away at a sharp angle into the ravine. The trees and I know each other quite intimately, and we have much to say to each other from time to time.

I do nearly all my writing at this window seat. The trees watch over me as I write. Whenever I look up, they remind me that they are there. They are my best critics. As long as I am aware of their presence, I can try to avoid the trivial and the banal.

Ramesh, the son of the municipal cleaner, looms darkly in the doorway. He is a stunted boy with a large head, but has wide gentle eyes. His orange-coloured trousers brighten up the surrounding gloom.

'What do you want, Ramesh?'

'Newspapers.'

'To sell to the kabari?'

'No. For wrapping my schoolbooks.'

'Well, take a few.' I give him half a dozen old newspapers, the headlines already look meaningless. 'Sit down and wait for it to stop raining.'

He sits awkwardly on a mora.

'And what is your cousin Vinod doing these days?' (Vinod is a good-looking ne'er-do-well who seldom does anything apart from hanging around cinema halls.)

'Nothing.'

'Doesn't he go to school?'

'He has stopped going to school. He got a job at fifty rupees a month, but he left after a week. He says he will join the army in September.'

The rain stops and Ramesh departs. The clouds begin to

break up, the sun strikes the steep hill on my left. A woman is chopping up sticks. I hear the tinkle of cowbells. Water drips from a leaking drainpipe. And suddenly, clear and pure, the song of the whistling thrush emerges like a dark sweet secret from the depths of the ravine.

Bijju is back from school and is taking his parents' cattle out to graze. He sees me at the window and waves, then grabs his favourite cow Neelu by the tail and tells her to hurry up.

Bijju is twelve, a fair, good-looking Garhwali boy. His younger sister and brother are very pretty children. The father, an electrician, is a rather self-effacing man. The mother is a strong, hard woman. I have watched her on the hillside cutting grass. She has the muscular calves of a man, solid feet and heavy hands; but she is a handsome woman. They live in a rented outhouse further up the hill.

Bijju doesn't visit me very often. He is rather shy. But one day I looked out of the window and there he was in the branches of the oak tree, smiling at me rather hesitantly. We spoke to each other across the three or four yards that separate house from oak tree.

'If I jump, I can land in your tree,' I said.

'And if I jump I will be in your house,' said Bijju.

'Come on then, jump!'

But he shook his head. He was afraid of me. The tree was safe. He put his arms round the thickest branch and held himself close to it. He looked very right in the tree, as though he belonged there, a boy of the woods, a tree spirit peeping out from a house of glossy new leaves.

'Come on, jump!'

'*You* jump,' he said.

In the evening his sister brings the cows home. I meet her

on the path above the house. She is only a year younger than Bijju, a very bonny girl who is going to be ravishingly beautiful when she grows up, if they don't marry her off too soon. She too has the same timid smile. But if these children are timid of humans, they are not afraid in the forest, and often wander far afield with Neelu the blue cow and others. (And S, who is eighteen and educated at an English-medium private school, wouldn't go alone into the forest if you paid him!) But the trees know their own. They will cherish the wild spirits and frighten the daylights out of the tame.

The whistling thrush is here, bathing in the rainwater puddle beneath the window. He loves this spot. So now, when there is no rain, I fill the puddle with water, just so that my favourite bird keeps coming.

His bath finished, he perches on a branch of the walnut tree. His glossy blue-black wings glitter in the sunshine. At any moment he will start singing.

Here he goes! He tries out the tune, whistling to himself, and then, confident of the notes, sends his thrilling full-throated voice far over the forest. The song dies down, trembling, lingering in the air; starts again, joyfully, and then suddenly stops, as though the singer had forgotten the words or the tune.

Vinod, the ne'er-do-well, turns up with a friend, asking me to give them some work. They want to go to the pictures but have no money.

'You can dig up this slope below the house,' I tell them. 'The soil is good for growing vegetables.'

This sounds too much like hard work for Vinod, who says, 'We'll come and do it tomorrow.'

'No, we'll do it now,' says his more enterprising friend, and to my surprise they set to work.

Now and then I look out of the window. They are digging away with fair enthusiasm.

After about half an hour, Vinod keeps sitting down for short rests, to the increasing irritation of his partner. They are soon snapping at each other. Vinod looks very funny when he sulks, because he has a snub nose, and somehow a snub nose and a ferocious expression only reminds me of Richmal Crompton's William. But the work gets done by evening and they are quite pleased with their earnings.

Bijju is right at the top of a big oak. The branches sway to his movements. He grins down at me and waves. The higher he is in the tree, the more confident he becomes. It is only when he is down on the ground that he becomes shy and speechless.

He has allowed the cows to wander, and presently his mother's deep voice can be heard calling, 'Neelu, Neelu!' (The other cows don't have names.) And then: 'Where is that wretched boy?'

Sir Edmund Gibson has come up. He spends the summer in the big house just down the road. He is wheezing a lot and says he has water in his lungs—and who wouldn't, at the age of eighty-six?

'Ruskin, my advice to you,' he says, 'is never to live beyond the age of eighty.'

'Well, once ought to be enough, sir.'

He is a big man, but not as red in the face as he used to be. His Gurkha manservant, Tirlok, has to push him up the steep slope to my gate.

Sir Edmund was once the British Resident in the Kathiawar states. He knew my parents in Jamnagar, when I was just five or six. He is a bachelor and is looked after by his servants.

His farm at Ramgarh doesn't make any money and he will

probably give it to his retainers.

When Sir Edmund was Resident, he was once shot at from close range by a terrorist. The man took four shots and missed every time. He must have been a terrible shot, or perhaps the pistol was faulty, because Sir E presents a very large target.

He also treasures two letters from Mahatma Gandhi, which were written from prison.

'I liked Gandhi,' says Sir E. 'He had a sense of humour. No politician today has a sense of humour. They all take themselves far too seriously. But not Gandhi. He took his work seriously, but not himself. When I went to see him in prison, I asked him if he was comfortable, and he smiled and said, "Even if I was, I wouldn't admit it!"'

Sir E's servant brings tea, but there isn't any milk. I think I have exhausted Bijju's supply.

Now it's dusk and the trees are very still, very quiet. Far away I can hear the *chuk-chuk-chuk* of a nightjar. The lights on Landour hill come on, one by one. Prem is singing in the kitchen. There is a whirr of wings as the king crows fly into the trees to roost for the night. A rustling in the dry leaves below the window. A snake? Field rats? Porcupines? It is now too dark to find out. The day has ended, and the trees move closer together in the dark.

We are treated to one of those spectacular electric storms which are fairly frequent at this time of the year, late spring or early summer. The clouds grow very dark, then send bolts of lightning sizzling across the sky, lighting up the entire range of mountains. When the storm is directly overhead, there is hardly a pause in the frequency of the lightning; it is like a bright light being switched on and off with barely a second's interruption.

John Lang, writing in Dickens's magazine *Household Words*

in 1853, almost exactly a hundred and twenty years ago, had this to say about one of our storms:

> I have seen a storm on the heights of Jura—such a storm as Lord Byron describes. I have seen lightning, and heard thunder in Australia; I have, off Tierra del Fuego, the Cape of Good Hope, and the coast of Java, kept watch in thunderstorms which have drowned in their roaring the human voice, and made everyone deaf and stupefied; but these storms are not to be compared with a thunderstorm at Mussoorie or Landour.

Forgotten today, Lang was a popular writer in the mid-nineteenth century. He was also a successful barrister, who represented the Rani of Jhansi in her litigation with the East India Company. He spent his last years in Mussoorie and was buried in the Camel's Back cemetery. His grave proved to be almost as elusive as his books and I found it with some difficulty, overgrown with moss and periwinkle. Prem and I cleaned it up until the inscription stood out quite clearly.

Prem won't come home on a stormy night like this. He is afraid of the dark, but more than that, he is afraid of thunderstorms. It is as though the gods are ganging up against him. So he will spend the night in the school quarters, where he is visiting his mother who is staying there with relatives.

In the morning he turns up with a sheepish grin, saying it got very late and he didn't want to wake me in the middle of the night. I try to feign anger, but it is a gloriously fresh and spirited morning; impossible to feel angry. A strong breeze is driving the clouds away, and the sun keeps breaking through The birds are particularly active. The king crows (who weren't here last year) seem to have taken up residence in the oaks. I don't know why they are called crows. They are slim, elegant black birds, with long forked tails, and their call, far from being a caw, is quite musical, though slightly metallic. The mynahs are very busy, very noisy, looking for a nesting site in the roof. The babblers are raking over fallen leaves, snapping up absent-minded grasshoppers. Now and then, the whistling thrush bursts into song, and then all other bird sounds pale into insignificance. Bijju has taken his cows to pasture and now scrambles up the hill, heading for home; he is late for school, and that is why he is in a hurry. He waves to me.

Both he and Prem have the high cheekbones and the deep-set eyes of the hill people. Prem, of course, is tall and dark. Bijju is small and fair; but he will grow into a sturdy young fellow.

The rain has driven the scorpions out of their rocks and crevices. I found one sitting on a loaf of bread. Up came his sting when we disturbed him. Prem tipped him out on the veranda steps and he scurried off into the bushes. I do not kill insects and other small creatures if I can help it, but there is a limit to my hospitality. I spared a centipede yesterday even though, last year, I was bitten by one which had occupied the seat of my pyjamas. Our hill scorpions and centipedes are not as dangerous as those found in the plains, and probably the same can be said for the people.

Prem tells me that his uncle is immune to scorpion stings, and allows himself to be stung in order to demonstrate his immunity. Apparently his mother was stung by a scorpion shortly before his birth!

◆

Azure butterflies flit about the garden like flakes of sky.

Learnt two new words: bosky = wooded, bushy (bosky

shadows); girding = jesting, jeering (girding schoolboys, girding monkeys).

Poor old Sir E is in a bad way. He has diarrhoea, and little or no control over the muscles that play a part in controlling the bowels. The Gurkha servant called me, and I went over with some tablets. Sir E looked quite exhausted and was panting from the exertion of walking from his bed to the toilet. The Gurkha is very good—gives Sir E his bath, dresses him, helps him on with his pyjamas.

Grateful for my alacrity in coming over with some medicine, Sir E offers me a whisky-and-soda (the first time he has ever done this), and pours himself a stiff brandy. He dozes off now and then, but the laboured breathing won't stop. He is a tough old tree, but I think he is beginning to find his massive frame something of a burden.

I make an attempt at conversation. 'Were you at Oxford or Cambridge?'

'Oxford. I joined Oxford in 1905 and left in 1909. Came out to India in 1910.'

He has an excellent memory, unlike Mr Biggs (a retired headmaster) who is ten years younger but will repeat the same story thrice in ten minutes.

And when were you knighted?' I ask.

'1939 or 1940.'

He is too tired to do much talking. I let him doze off, and give my attention to the whisky. The log fire burns well, the flames cast their glow on Sir E's white hair and hanging jowls. The stertorous breathing grows in volume. He wakes up suddenly, complains that the fire is too hot; Tirlok opens the window. I finish the whisky; he doesn't offer another. It is his supper time, anyway, and I suggest soup and toast. 'Call me in the night if you have any trouble,' I say. He looks very grateful. The loneliness must press upon him a great deal.

I go out into the night. The trees are bending to a strong wind. From the foliage comes a deep sigh, the voice of leagues of trees sleeping and half disturbed in their sleep. The sky is clear, tremendous with stars.

For the first time this year I hear the barbet, a sure sign the summer is upon us. Its importunate cry carries far across the hills. It can keep this up for hours, like a beggar. Indeed, its plaint—*un-neow, un-neow!*—has been likened in the hills to that of the spirit of the village moneylender who has died before he can collect his dues. (*'Un-neow!'* is a cry for justice!)

It is difficult to spot the barbet. It is a fat green bird (no bigger than a mynah, but fatter), and it usually perches at the very top of a deodar or cypress.

The whistling thrush comes to bathe in the rainwater puddle. Sir E is much better and is sitting outside in the shade of an old oak. They are probably about the same age. What a rugged constitution this man must have; first, to survive, as a young man, all those diseases such as cholera, typhoid, dysentery, malaria, even the plague, which carried off so many Europeans in India (including my father); and now, an old man, to live and battle with congested lungs, a bad heart, weak eyes, bad teeth, recalcitrant bowels, and god knows what else, and still be able to derive some pleasure from living. His old Hillman car is equally indestructible. But, like Sir E, it can't get up the hill any more; he uses it only in Dehradun.

I think his longevity is due simply to the fact that he refuses to go to bed when he is unwell. No amount of diarrhoea, or water in his lungs, will prevent him from getting up, dressing, writing letters, or getting on with the latest Wodehouse (a contemporary of his) or *Blackwood's Magazine*, to which he has been subscribing for the last fifty years! He was pleased to find that some of my own essays were appearing in *Blackwood's*. Nothing will keep him from his four o'clock tea or his evening whisky-and-soda. He is determined, I am sure, to die in his chair, with all his clothes on. The thought of being taken unawares while still in his pyjamas must be something of a nightmare to him. (His favourite film, he once told me, was *They Died With Their Boots On*.)

The cicadas are tuning up for their first summer concert. Even Mrs Biggs, who is hard of hearing, can hear them. Yesterday I met her on the road above the cottage and exchanged pleasantries. Up at Wynberg the girls' choir was hard at practice.

'The girls are in good voice today,' I remarked.

'Oh yes, Mr Bond,' she said, presuming I meant the cicadas. 'They do it with their legs, don't they?'

A week in Delhi. It is still only early summer, but the heat almost knocks one over. Slept on a roof, along with thousands of mosquitoes. It cools off in the early hours, but only briefly, before the sun comes shouting over the rooftops. The dust lies thick on floors, leaves, books, people. May's golden dust!

Now, back in the hills, I am struck first of all by the silence. The house, too, makes itself felt. It has been here too long not to have acquired a personality of its own. It is not a cheerful-looking place, nor is it exactly gloomy. My bedroom is rather dark (because it faces the abrupt slope of the hillside), but there is a wild cherry growing just outside the window—a cherry tree which I nurtured ever since it was a tiny seedling, five or six years ago, and which has now grown so tall that the branches tap against the roof whenever there is a breeze. It is a funny sort of cherry because it flowers in November instead of in the spring like other fruit trees. Small birds and small boys willingly eat the berries, which are too acid for adult palates.

The sitting room, with its two big windows looking out on the forest, is a bright room. Most of the wall space is taken up by my books. The rugs are worn and tattered—they have been with the house right from the beginning, I think—and I can't afford new ones.

> On books and friends I spend my money;
> For stones and bricks I haven't any.

Sir E, quite recovered from his recent illness, has gone down to Dehra again to attend to his farm and the demands of his farm workers. He should be back at the end of the month.

The brilliant blue-black of the whistling thrush shows up best when the sun is glinting off its back, but this seldom happens, because the bird likes to keep to the shade where it is almost black. Hopping about, it reminds me of Fred Astaire dancing in tophat and tails.

Now that it's getting hot, my small pool attracts a number of afternoon visitors—the mynahs, babblers, a bulbul, a magpie. After their dip they perch in the cherry tree to dry themselves and I can watch them without getting up from my bed, where I take an afternoon siesta. I reserve the afternoons for doing nothing. 'Silence and non-action are the root of all things,' says Tao. Especially on a drowsy afternoon.

But I haven't seen the whistling thrush for several days. Perhaps he is offended at having to share the pool which he was the first to discover. I haven't heard his song either, which probably means that he has moved down to the stream where it is cooler and shadier.

Prem's mother and younger sister come for a few days.

His mother is a very quiet woman and doesn't say much even to her son. She is quite handsome, although she looks rather worn and tired, due probably to her recent illness.

His little sister, about four, is a friendly little gazelle; not in the least pretty, but lively and intelligent. She will have to stay here for at least six months to be properly treated for her incipient tuberculosis. There is no treatment to be had in their village.

While I am resting, still exhausted from an attack of hill dysentery (who called this a health resort?), Sir E blows in, red-faced, as distressed as a stranded whale. His Gurkha servant has walked out, after quarrelling with his wife and mother-in-law, and has taken with him his twin sons (aged one and a half). I calm Sir E, tell him Tirlok will be back in a day or two—he is probably trying to show how indispensable he is!

Sir E takes out a cigarette and strikes a match, and the entire matchbox flares up, burning a finger. Definitely not his day. I apply Burnol.

'It's all that damned girl's fault,' he says. 'She has a vile temper, just like her mother. We were very wise not to marry, Ruskin.'

Wise or not, I seem to have acquired a family all the same.

◆

Hundreds of white butterflies are flitting through the forest.

When Prem told his mother that I kept a human skull in my sitting room (given to me by Anil, a medical student, and *not* pinched from the cemetery as some suppose), she told him not to spend too much time near it. If he did, he would be possessed by the spirit of the woman who had originally inhabited the skull.

But Prem, at the present time, is immune to spirits, having succumbed to the charms of his young wife who stays downstairs with his mother. They have only been married a few months. He leans over the balcony, chatting with her; advises her on how to keep the courtyard clean; then makes her a small broom from the twigs of a wild honeysuckle bush. She enjoys all the attention she is getting.

The sky is overcast this morning. Dust from the plains has formed a thick haze which hides the valley and the mountains. We are badly in need of rain. Down in the plains, over two hundred people have died of heatstroke.

I haven't seen Bijju for some days, but this morning his sister, Binya, was out with the cows. What a sturdy little girl she is; and pretty, too. I will write a story about her.[1]

'We'll take you to the pictures one day, Sir Edmund.'

'Yes, I must see one more picture before I die.'

So there comes a time when we start thinking in terms of the last picture, the last book, the last visit, the last party. But Sir E's remark is matter of fact. He is given to boredom but not to melancholy.

And he has a timeless quality. I have noticed this in other old people; they look more permanent than the young.

He sums it all up by saying, 'I don't mind being dead, but I shall miss being alive.'

A number of small birds are here to bathe and drink in the little pool beneath the cherry tree: hunting parties of tits—grey tits, red-headed tits and green-backed tits—and two delicate little willow warblers. They take turns in the pool. While the green-backs are taking a plunge, the red-heads wait patiently on the moss-covered rocks, coming down later to sip daintily at the edge of the pool; they don't like getting their feet wet! Finally,

[1]This story was called 'The Blue Umbrella'.

when they have all gone away, the whistling thrush arrives and indulges in an orgy of bathing, as he now has the entire pool to himself.

The babblers are adept at snapping up the little garden skinks that scuttle about in the leaves and grass. The skinks are quite brittle and are easily broken to pieces with a few hard raps of the beak. Then down they go! Babblers are also good at sifting through dead leaves and seizing upon various insects.

The honeybees push their way through the pursed lips of the antirrhinum and disappear completely. A few minutes later they stagger out again, bottoms first.

◆

1 June

The dry spell continues. It is only before sunrise that there is any freshness in the air.

At dawn I said, 'Day, you will not begin without me.' I was up with the whistling thrush at five. The cicadas were tuning up, the crickets were already in full cry, and the whistling thrush was calling most sweetly. As none of these songsters could be seen, it was as though the forest itself was singing.

Feeling the dawn wind stir, I was happy that I had met the day at its very beginning.

When the sun came up, the day became sultry and oppressive. I had to walk two miles to Ban Suman and back. There was no shade anywhere along the road. But we are equipped with legs for the purpose of walking. As more and more people grow dependent on their cars, a new species of humans will evolve. Around the turn of the twenty-second century, I can see legless humans being born. By then, of course, there will be flying wheelchairs.

A pall of dust hangs over the mountain.

Someone asked Sir E if he could shoot a bird on his land at Ramgarh. The man wanted the bird for dissection in a biology lab. Sir E refused.

'It's in the interests of science,' protested the man. 'Do you think a bird is better than a human?'

'Infinitely,' said Sir E. 'Infinitely better.'

He goes down today to pay his farmhands. He will return in a few days unless it gets cooler in Dehra. He complains of being very bored up here, for he can't get about, and in Dehra he has his Hillman. 'I'm *rotting* with boredom,' he says.

Vinod, I hear, is laid low with a fever—the result of a day's hard work. He is now in retirement for the rest of the season.

Walked five miles down the Tehri road to Suakholi, where I rested in a small tea shop, a loose stone structure with a tin roof held down by stones. It serves the bus passengers, mule drivers, milkmen and others who use this road.

I find a couple of mules tethered to a pine tree. The mule drivers, handsome men in tattered clothes, sit on a bench in the shade of the tree, drinking tea from brass tumblers. The shopkeeper, a man of indeterminate age—the cold dry winds from the mountain passes having crinkled his face like a walnut—greets me enthusiastically, as he always does. He even produces a chair, which looks like a survivor from the Savoy's 1890 ballroom. Fortunately the Mussoorie antique dealers haven't seen it, or it would have been carried away long ago. In any case, the stuffing has come out of the seat. The shopkeeper apologizes for its condition: 'The rats were nesting in it.' And then, to reassure me: 'But they have gone now.'

Unlike the shopkeeper, the mule drivers have somewhere to go and something to deliver: sacks of potatoes. From Jaunpur to Jaunsar, the potato is probably the crop best suited to these stony, terraced fields. Oddly enough, it was introduced to the Himalayas by two Irishmen, Captain Young of Dehra and Mussoorie and Captain Kennedy of Simla, in the 1820s. The slopes of Young's house, Mullingar, were known as his Potato Farm. Looking up old books, I was surprised to learn that the potato wasn't known in India before the nineteenth century, and now it's an essential part of our diet in most parts of the country.

As the mule drivers lead their pack animals away, along the dusty road to Landour bazaar, I follow at a distance, singing 'Mule Train' in my best Nelson Eddy manner.[2]

A thunderstorm, followed by strong winds, brought down the temperature. That was yesterday. And today, June, it is cloudy, cool, drizzling a little, almost monsoon weather; but it is still too early for the real monsoon.

The birds are enjoying the cool weather. The green-backed tits cool their bottoms in the rainwater pool. A king crow flashes past, winging through the air like an arrow. On the wing, it snaps up a hovering dragonfly. The mynahs fetch crow feathers to line their nest in the eaves of the house. I am lying so still on the window seat that a tit alights on the sill within a few inches of my head. It snaps up a small dead moth before flying away.

Sir E is back. He found it too hot in the valley. Even up here he has given up wearing a necktie. I'll have him wearing a kurta and pyjamas before long; the only sensible dress in summer.

At dusk I sit at the window and watch the trees and listen to the wind as it makes light conversation in the leafy tops of the maples. A large bat flits in and out of the trees. The sky is just light enough to enable me to see the bat and the

---

[2]Not Nelson's song originally, but he sang it better than anyone else.

outlines of the taller trees. Up on Landour hill, the lights are just beginning to come on. It is deliciously cool, eight o'clock, a perfect summer's evening. Prem is singing to himself in the kitchen. His wife and sister are chattering beneath the walnut tree. Down the hill, a kakar is barking, alarmed perhaps by the presence of a leopard. All the birds have gone to sleep for the night. Even the cicadas are strangely silent. The wind grows stronger and the tall maples bow before it: the maple moves its slender branches slowly from side to side, the oak moves its branches up and down. It is darker now; more lights on Landour. The cry of the barking deer has grown fainter, more distant, and now I hear a cricket singing in the bushes. The stars are out, the wind grows chilly, it is time to close the window.

Bijju is very much an outdoor boy, even when he isn't grazing cows. He isn't very strong in the chest, but his legs are sturdy; he was having no difficulty in scaling the high retaining wall. He grinned down at me. He is rather like the whistling thrush—absent for days, then unexpectedly reappearing in the forest or on the hillside. Bijju sings too, although his voice is more vigorous than melodic.

And that reminds me of the story of the whistling thrush. The bird was once a village boy who tried very hard to play the flute in the same style as the god Krishna. When the god heard his favourite melody being plagiarized, he was furious and turned the unfortunate boy into a bird. The whistling thrush still tries to copy the divine melody, but somehow it always breaks off right in the middle of a stanza. There ought to be a moral here, especially in a land full of plagiarists. Or to be fair, I should say film-land...

The Whistler. This is my name for the youth who labours part-time in the school. He is something of a character—

scatterbrained, carefree, easy-going. He is always whistling—loudly and quite tunefully (this time a bird turned into a boy?)—so that you know when he's coming round a bend or through the trees, and even when it's dark you know who it is. He's usually out quite late, because he spends all his money at the pictures. He has three sisters, and they and the mother are all working as maids or ayahs, and as they are quite indulgent to him (the only brother) he doesn't have to work too hard. His shoes are always torn, even though his clothes look new.

He has a reputation for being a waster, but he returned the few rupees he borrowed from me last month. I suppose a youth who is always singing and whistling on the roads gives everyone the impression that he has nothing to do from morn till night, unlike that jolly miller of Dee who worked *and* sang the whole day through. (I know one man who forbids his children from singing in the home.)

But back to the Whistler, he is really quite enterprising. The other day he asked me for one of my books, and as I knew he hadn't squandered too many years in school, I gave him an easy Hindi translation of one of my children's books. But it was the paper he valued, not the words. He flogged it to the bania's small son, who took it apart and converted the large pages into envelopes, which were then used for selling gram and peanuts. In India it doesn't take long for anything to be recycled. On the way home, I saw a couple of customers throwing their empty packets away, and these were promptly consumed by a stray cow. There went my beautiful story!

Is there a lesson to be learnt from this? Yes. Don't give away complimentaries.

It rained all night, and the morning is cool and fresh. Parrots are on the wing. I feel like tap-dancing like Gene Kelly, but you can't tap dance on a hillside, you'd break an ankle. Only the roads (and not all of them) are suitable for a song-and-dance act, and no doubt the Whistler will oblige before long. At forty, I must refrain from being too frisky and boyish. But I'll do a reel in the garden when no one is looking.

◆

24 June

The first day of monsoon mist. And it's strange how all the birds fall silent as the mist comes climbing up the hill. Perhaps that's what makes the mist so melancholy; not only does it conceal the hills, it blankets them in silence too. Only an hour ago the trees were ringing with birdsong. And now the forest is deathly still, as though it were midnight.

Through the mist Bijju is calling to his sister. I can hear him running about on the hillside but I cannot see him.

Feeling sorry for Sir E (or maybe for myself), I walked over to see him. The door was closed, so I looked in at the French window (nothing could be more *English* than a French window, and no Agatha Christie mystery would be complete without one), I saw him sleeping in his chair with his chin on his chest. There was no dagger sticking out of his back, only a bit of stuffing from his old coat. My footsteps on the gravel woke him, and he got up and opened the door for me. He said he felt a bit tipsy; had taken his usual peg, but thought the quality of whisky varied from bottle to bottle, and wished he could lay his hands on a bottle of Scotch or even Irish. He could only offer me an Uttar Pradesh brand. I said I'd given up drinking, and this pleased him because in truth he hates anyone drinking his whisky; said he might give it up himself, it 'cost too damn much'! I told him it would be unwise to give up drinking at this stage of his life. As he had reached the age of eighty-six on two pegs a day, he was obviously thriving on it. Giving it up now would only play havoc with the orderly working of his system. I'd given it up in order to help an alcoholic friend abstain, and also because I wanted to give up *something*, and strong drink seemed the easiest thing to do without.

A cicada starts up in the tree nearest my window seat. What has he been doing all these weeks, and why does he choose this particular moment and this particular evening to play the fiddle so loudly? The cicadas are late this year, the monsoon has been late. But soon the forest will be ringing with the sound of the cicadas—an orchestra constantly tuning up but never quite getting into tune—and the sound of the birds will be pushed into the background.

Outside the front door I found an elegant young praying mantis reclining on a leaf of the honeysuckle creeper. I say young because he hadn't grown to his full size, and was that very tender pale green which is the colour of a young mantis. They are light brown to begin with, like dry twigs, but as they grow older and the monsoon foliage becomes greener, they too change, and by mid-August they are dark green.

As though to make up for lost time, the monsoon rains are now here with a vengeance. It has been pouring all day, and already the roof is leaking. But nothing dampens Prem's spirits. He is still singing love songs in the kitchen.

Kailash, whom I have known for a couple of weeks, asks me for twenty-five rupees.

'What do you need it for?' I ask.

'It's for my Sanskrit teacher,' he says. 'I have failed in Sanskrit but if I give the teacher twenty-five rupees he'll alter my marks. You see, I've passed in all the other subjects, but if I fail in

Sanskrit I'll fail the entire exam and remain a pre-Inter student for another year.'

I took a little time to digest this information and ponder on the pitfalls of the examination system.

'He must be failing a lot of boys,' I said. 'Twenty-five rupees each! Are there many others?'

'Some. But he dare not fail the good ones. They can ask for a recheck. It's the borderline cases like me who give him a chance to make money.'

This placed me in a quandary. Should I yield to the evils of the examination system and provide the money for pass-marks? Or should I adopt a high moral stance and allow the boy to fail?

Whatever the evils of the exam system, they are not the fault of the student. And either way he isn't going to turn into a great Sanskrit scholar. So why be a hypocrite? I gave him the money.

Kailash slogs in his uncle's orchard all morning, gets a midday meal (no breakfast), and hasn't any shoes. And yet his uncle, a member of one of Garhwal's well-known upper-caste families, is a wealthy man.

Kailash tells me he will return to his village once he knows his result. According to him his uncle is such a miser that at mealtimes he pauses before each mouthful, wondering: 'Ought I to eat it? Or should I keep it for tomorrow?'

I am visited by another kind of student, a small girl from one of the private schools. Her mother has brought her to me for my autograph.

'She studies your book in class six,' I was informed.

'And what book is that?' I asked the little girl.

'*Tom Sawyer,*' she replied promptly. So I signed for Mark Twain. When a small storeroom collapsed during the last heavy rains, I was forced to rescue a couple of old packing cases that had been left there for three or four years—since my arrival here, in fact. The contents were well soaked and most of it had to be thrown away—old manuscripts that had been obliterated, negatives that had got stuck together, gramophone records that had taken on strange shapes (dear 'Ink Spots', how will I ever listen to you again?[3])... Unlike most writers, I have no compunction about throwing away work that hasn't quite come off, and I am sure there are a few critics who would prefer that I throw away the lot! Sentimental rubbish, no doubt. Well, we can't please everyone; and we can't preserve everything either. Time and the elements will take their toll.

But a couple of old diaries, kept in exercise books almost twenty years ago, had managed to survive the rain, and I put them out in the sun to dry, and then, almost unwillingly, started browsing through them. It was instructive, and sometimes a little disconcerting, to discover the sort of person I had been in my twenties. In some ways, no different from what I am today. In other ways, radically different. A diary is a useful tool for self-examination, particularly if both diary and diarist are still around after some years.

One particular entry caught my eye, and I reproduce it here without any alteration, because it represented my credo as a young writer, and it set me wondering if I had lived up to my own expectations. (Nobody else had any expectations of me!)

The entry was made on 19 January 1958, when I was living on my own in Dehradun:

> The things I do best are those things I do on my own, alone, of my own accord, without the advice or approval of others. Once I start doing what other people tell me

---

[3]This was before the advent of audiotapes.

> to do, both my character and creativity take a dip. It is when I strike out on my own that I succeed best.
>
> There was a time when I was much younger and poorer than I am now. I had been over a year in Jersey, in the Channel Islands; I was unhappy, and the atmosphere in which I was writing was one of discouragement and disapproval. And that was why I wrote so well—because I was defiant! That was why I finished the only book I have finished so far. I had to prove to myself that I could do it.
>
> One night I was walking alone along the beach. There was a strong wind blowing, dashing the salt spray in my face, and the sea was crashing against the St Helier rocks. I told myself: I will go to London; I will take up a job; I will finish my book; I will find a publisher; I will save money and I will return to India, because I can be happier there than here.
>
> And that was just what I did.
>
> I had guts then.
>
> What's more, I had an end in view.
>
> The writing itself is not enough for me. Success and money are not enough. I had a little of both recently,[4] but they did not help me to do anything wonderful. I must have something to write for, just as I must have something to live for. And that's something I have yet to find.

There was more in that vein, but I give this excerpt as an example of a young man's determination to be a writer in what were then adverse circumstances. Thirty-five years later, I'm still trying.

---

[4]When *The Room on the Roof* was published (1956).

◆

27 June

The rains have heralded the arrival of some seasonal visitors—a leopard; and several thousand leeches.

Yesterday afternoon the leopard lifted a dog from near the servants' quarters below the school. In the evening it attacked one of Bijju's cows but fled at the approach of Bijju's mother, who came screaming imprecations.

As for the leeches, I shall soon get used to a little bloodletting every day. Bijju's mother sat down in the shrubbery to relieve herself, and later discovered two fat black leeches feeding on her fair round bottom. I told her she could use one of the spare bathrooms downstairs. But she prefers the wide open spaces.

Other new arrivals are the scarlet minivets (the females are yellow), flitting silently among the leaves like brilliant jewels. No matter how leafy the trees, these brightly coloured birds cannot conceal themselves, although, by remaining absolutely silent, they sometimes contrive to go unnoticed. Along come a pair of drongos, unnecessarily aggressive, chasing the minivets away.

A tree creeper moves rapidly up the trunk of the oak tree, snapping up insects all the way. Now that the rains are here, there is no dearth of food for the insectivorous birds.

In spite of there being water in several places, the whistling thrush still comes to my pool. He, at least, is a permanent resident.

Kailash has a round, cheerful face, only slightly marred by a swivel eye. His hair comes down over his forehead, hiding a deep scar. He is short, but quite compact and energetic. He chatters a good deal but in a general sort of way, and a response isn't obligatory.

It's quite possible that he will go away as soon as he gets

his exam results. He's fed up with being the Cinderella of his uncle's house. He tells of how his miserly uncle went to see a rather permissive film, and was very shocked and wanted to walk out, but couldn't bear the thought of losing his ticket money; so he sat through the film with his eyes closed.

Sir E departed for Dehra with his large retinue of servants and their dependants, all of whom would have done justice to an eighteenth-century nabob. 'I am at the mercy of my servants,' he told me the other day.

But he had placed himself at their mercy long ago, by setting himself up as a country squire surrounded by 'faithful retainers'—all of whom received generous salaries but did little or no work. If he sold his white elephant of a farm, he'd be quite comfortable with one servant.

'I'll probably come up in September, after the rains,' he said. 'If I live that long... I'm just living from day to day.'

'So am I,' I told him. 'It's the best way to live.'

A couple of days passed before Kailash came to see me. I was beginning to wonder if he'd come again. Apparently the teacher had at first proved elusive; but the deed was done, and Kailash passed with the marks he needed. Ironically, his uncle was so impressed that he is now urging the boy to remain with him and complete the Intermediate exam.

'I must write a story about your uncle,' I remark.

'Don't give him a story', says Kailash. 'A short note will do.'

Now that Prem is preoccupied with his wife, and the house is at the mercy of uninvited visitors, I stay out most of the time, and these days Kailash is my only companion. Yesterday we took Camel's Back Road, past the cemetery. He chatters away, and I can listen if I want to, or think of other things if I don't want to listen; apparently it makes no difference to him.

He is a cheerful soul, with an infectious laugh. He walks with a slight swagger, or roll. He says he doesn't mind staying here now that he has me for a friend; that he can put up with two sour uncles as long as he knows I'm around. I suspect he's quite capable of pulling a fast one on his uncle; but all the same, I find myself liking him.

Moody. And when I'm moody I'm bad.

Prem says: 'It is easier to please God than it is to please you.'

'But God is easily pleased,' I respond. 'God makes absolutely no demands on us. We just imagine them.'

The eyes.

Prem's eyes have great gentleness in them.

His wife's eyes are round and mischievous and suggestive…

Suggestive enough to invite the attention of a mischievous or malignant spirit.

At about two in the morning I am awakened by Prem's shouts, muffled by rain. Shouting back that I am on my way, for it is obviously an emergency, I leap out of bed, grab an umbrella, dash outside and then down the stairs to his room. His wife is sobbing in bed. Whatever had possessed her has now gone away, and the crying is due more to Prem's ministrations—he exorcizes the ghost by thumping her on the head—than to the 'possession' itself. But there is no doubt that she is subject to hallucinatory or subconscious actions. It is not simply a hysterical fit. She walks in her sleep, moves restlessly from door to window, holds conversations with an invisible presence, and resists all efforts to bring her back to reality. When she comes out of the trance, she is quite normal.

This sort of thing is apparently quite common in the hills, where people believe it to be a ghost taking temporary possession of a human mind. It's happened to Prem's wife before, and it also happens to her brother, so it seems to run in families. It never happens to Prem, who deeply resents the interruption to his sleep.

I calm the girl and then make them bring their bedding upstairs. I give her a sleeping tablet and she is soon fast asleep.

During a lull in the rain, I hear a most hideous sound coming from the forest—a maniacal shrieking, followed by a mournful hooting. But Prem and his wife sleep through it all. The rain starts again, and the shrieking stops. Perhaps it's a hyena. Perhaps something else.

A morning of bright sunshine, and the whistling thrush welcomes it with a burst of song. Where do the birds shelter when it rains? How does that frail butterfly survive the battering of strong winds and heavy raindrops? How do the snakes manage in their flooded holes?

I saw a bright green snake sunning itself on some rocks; no doubt waiting for its hole to dry out.

In my vagrant days, ten to fifteen years ago (long before the hippies made vagrancy a commonplace), I was a great frequenter of tea shops, those dingy little shacks with a table and three chairs, a grimy tea kettle, and a cracked gramophone. Tea shops haven't changed much, and once again I find myself lingering in them, sometimes in company with Kailash, who, although he doesn't eat much, drinks a lot of tea.

One can sit all day in a tea shop and watch the world go by. Amazing the number of people who actually do this! And not all of them unemployed. The tea shop near the clock tower is ideal for this purpose. It is a busy part of the bazaar but the tea shop, though small, is gloomy within, and one can loll about unseen, observing everyone who passes by a few feet away in the sunlit (or rain-spattered) street. The tea itself is indifferent, the buns are stale, the boiled eggs have been peppered too liberally. Kailash is unusually quiet; there is no one else in the shop. People who would stop me in the road pass by without glancing into the murky interior. This is the ideal place; not as noble as my window opening into the trees, but familiar, reminiscent of days gone by in Dehra, when cares sat lightly upon me simply because I did not care at all. And now perhaps I have begun to care too much.

I gave Bijju a cake. He licked all the icing off it, only then did he eat the rest.

It was a dark windy corner in Landour bazaar, but I always found the old man there, hunched up over the charcoal fire on which he roasted his peanuts. He'd been there for as long as I could remember, and he could be seen at almost any hour of the day or night. Summer or winter, he stayed close to his fire.

He was probably quite tall, but we never saw him standing up. One judged his height from his long, loose limbs. He was very thin, and the high cheekbones added to the tautness of his tightly stretched skin.

His peanuts were always fresh, crisp and hot. They were popular with the small boys who had a few paise to spend on their way to and from school, and with the patrons of the cinemas, many of whom made straight for the windy corner during intervals or when the show was over. On cold winter evenings, or misty monsoon days, there was always a demand for the old man's peanuts.

No one knew his name. No one had ever thought of asking him for it. One just took him for granted. He was as fixed a landmark as the clock tower or the old cherry tree that grew crookedly from the hillside. The tree was always being lopped; the clock often stopped. The peanut vendor seemed less perishable than the tree, more dependable than the clock.

He had no family, but in a way all the world was his family, because he was in continuous contact with people. And yet he was a remote sort of being; always polite, even to children, but never familiar. There is a distinction to be made between aloneness and loneliness. The peanut vendor was seldom alone; but he must have been lonely.

Summer nights he rolled himself up in a thin blanket and slept on the ground, beside the dying embers of his fire. During the winter, he waited until the last show was over, before retiring to the rickshaw-coolies' shed where there was some protection from the biting wind.

Did he enjoy being alive? I wonder now. He was not a joyful person; but then, neither was he miserable. I should think he was a genuine stoic, one of those who do not attach overmuch importance to themselves, who are emotionally uninvolved, content with their limitations, their dark corners. I wanted to get to know the old man better, to sound him out on the immense questions involved in roasting peanuts all his life; but it's too late now. The last time I visited the bazaar the dark corner was deserted; the old man had vanished; the coolies had carried him down to the cremation ground.

'He died in his sleep,' said the tea-shop owner. 'He was very old.'

Very old. Sufficient reason to die.

But that corner is very empty, very dark, and whenever I pass it I am haunted by visions of the old peanut vendor, troubled by the questions I failed to ask; and I wonder if he was really as indifferent to life as he appeared to be.

Prem brought his wife some of her favourite mangoes. This afternoon he took her into my room so that she could listen to the radio. They both fell asleep at opposite ends of the bed; are still asleep as I write this in the next room, at my window. If I curled up a little, I could fall asleep here on the window seat. Nothing would induce me to disturb those innocents; they look far too blissful in their slumbers.

Kailash and I are caught in a storm and it's by far the worst storm of the year. To make matters worse, there is absolutely no shelter for a mile along the main road from the town. It was fierce, lashing rain, quite cold, whipping along on the wind from all angles. The road was soon a torrent of muddy water, as earth and stones came rushing down the hillsides. Our one umbrella was useless and was very nearly blown away. The cardboard carton in which we were carrying vegetables was soon reduced to pulp. We broke into a run, although we could hardly see our way. There were blinding flashes of lightning—is an umbrella a good or a bad conductor of electricity? Kailash sees humour in these situations and was in peals of laughter all the way home, even when we slid into a ditch.

He takes my hand and holds it between his hands. He is happy. He has got his self-confidence back, and can now deal with his uncles and Sanskrit teachers.

In the morning I work on a story. There is a dove cooing in the garden. Now it is very quiet, the only sound is the distant tapping of a woodpecker. The trees are muffled in ferns and creepers. It is mid-monsoon.

Kailash, his hair falling in an untidy mop across his forehead, drags me out of the house and over the wet green grass on the hillside. I protest that I do not like leeches, so we make for the high rocks. He laughs, talks, chuckles, and when he grins his large front teeth make him look like a 1940s' Mickey Rooney. When he looks sullen (this happens when he talks about his uncle), he looks Brando-ish. He has the gift of being able to convey his effervescence to me. Am I, at thirty-eight, too old to be gambolling about on the hill slopes like a young colt? (Am I, sobering thought, going to be a character of enforced youthfulness like the man on the boat in *Death in Venice*? Well, better that than the Gissing hero of *New Grub Street* who's old at forty.) If I am fit enough to gambol, then I must gambol. If I can still climb a tree, then I must climb trees, instead of just watching them from my window. I was in such high spirits yesterday that I kept playing the clown, and I haven't done this in years. To walk in the rain was fun, and to get wet was fun, and to fall down was fun, and to get hurt was fun.

'Will it last?' asks Kailash.

'This feeling of love between us?'

'*This* won't last. Not in this way. But if something *like* it lasts, we should be happy.'

Prem is happy, laughing, giggling all the time. Sometimes it is a little annoying for me, because he is obviously unaware of what is happening around him—such as the fact that part of the roof blew away in the storm—but I am a good Taoist, I say nothing, I wait for the right moment! Besides, it's a crime to interfere with anyone's happiness.

Prem notices the roof is missing and scolds his wife for seeing too many pictures. 'She's seen ten pictures in two months. More than she'd seen in her whole life, before coming here.' She pulls a face. Says Prem: 'My grandfather will be here any day to take her home.'

'Then she can see pictures with your grandfather,' I venture. 'While we repair the roof.'

'I wouldn't go anywhere with that old man,' she says.

'Don't speak like that of my grandfather. Do you want a beating? Look at Binya'—we all look at Binya, who is perched very prettily on the wall—'she hasn't seen more than two pictures in her life!'

'I'll take her to the pictures,' I offer.

Binya gives me a radiant smile. She'd love to go to the pictures, but her mother won't allow it.

Prem relents and takes his wife to the pictures.

Binya's mother has a bad attack of hiccups. Serves her right, for stealing my walnuts and not letting me take Binya to the pictures.

In the evening I find Prem teaching his wife the alphabet, using the kitchen door as a blackboard. It is covered with chalk marks. Love is teaching your wife to read and write!

◆

These entries were made in 1973, twenty years ago.

The following year I did not keep a journal, but these are some of the things that happened:

Sir E had a stroke and, like a stranded whale, finally heaved his last breath. According to his wishes, he was cremated on his farm near Dehra.

To Prem and Chandra was born a son, Rakesh, who immediately stole my heart—and gave me many a sleepless night, for as a baby he cried lustily.

Kailash went into the army and disappeared from my life, as well as from his uncle's.

Bijju and Binya were to remain a part of the hillside for several years.

Night of the Leopard

1

IN THE ENTIRE VILLAGE, RAKI WAS THE FIRST TO GET UP. EVEN THE dog, a large black mongrel called Raja, was asleep in a comer of the dark room, curled up near the embers of last night's fire. Raki's tousled head emerged from his blanket. He rubbed the sleep from his eyes and sat up. Then he crawled towards the loud ticking that came from the battered little clock which stood in a niche in the wall.

Bringing his face close to the clock, Raki could just make out the dial-hands. It was five o'clock. He had half an hour in which to get ready.

He got up, in undershirt and shorts, and moved quietly towards the door. The soft tread of his bare feet woke Raja, and the black dog rose silently and padded behind the boy. The door opened and closed, and boy and dog were outside in the chill dawn.

It was June, midsummer in the Himalayan valleys, but there was fresh dew on the grass. Raki felt the dew beneath his feet.

He took a deep breath and began walking down to the stream.

The sound of the stream filled the small valley. At that early hour it was the only sound but Raki was hardly conscious of it. It was a sound he lived with and took for granted. Only when the stream was too far away to be heard did he really miss its sound.

He slipped out of his clothes, gazed for a few moments at the goose pimples rising on his flesh, and then dashed into the shallow stream. The cold mountain water made him gasp with shock and delight. He moved slowly with the current and swam across to a small pool, where he plunged beneath the water.

The dog disliked cold water at that early hour. So he contented himself with sitting on a smooth rock and watching Raki as he splashed about in the clear water.

When Raki ran back to the house, he found his mother up, making tea and chapatties. His sister, Puja, was still asleep. She was two years older than Raki, a pretty girl with large black eyes. During the day, she helped her mother in the house and in the fields. She did not go to school with Raki. But when he came home in the evenings, he would teach her some of the things he had learnt. Their father was dead. Raki, at twelve, considered himself the head of the family.

He ate two chapatties, after spreading butter-oil on them. He drank a glass of hot sweet tea. His mother gave two of the thick flour-cakes to Raja, who wolfed them down. Then she wrapped two chapatties and a gourd-curry in some big green leaves and handed them to Raki. This was his lunch. His mother and Puja would eat afterwards.

Wearing a white shirt and black shorts and a pair of worn white gym shoes, he was ready for his long walk to school, five miles up the mountain.

Puja woke up just as he was about to leave. She pushed the hair away from her face and gave Raki one of her rare smiles.

'I hope you have not forgotten,' she said.

'Forgotten?' said Raki, pretending to sound puzzled. 'Is there something should remember?'

'Don't tease me. You promised to buy me a pair of bangles, remember? I hope you won't spend the money on sweets, as you did last time.'

'Oh yes, your bangles,' said Raki. 'Girls have nothing better to do than waste money on bangles. Now, don't lose your temper! I'll get them for you. Red and gold are the colours you want?'

'Yes, brother,' said Puja gently, pleased that Raki had remembered the colours. 'And for your dinner tonight we'll make something special. Won't we, mother?'

'All right, but hurry up and dress. We have to cut grass for the cows.'

They spoke in their own hill dialect, although sometimes Raki, to be wordly, would use an English or Hindi word.

His mother was winding the old clock. The sun would be up any minute.

Raki shouldered his schoolbag, kissed his mother, pinched his sister's cheeks, and left the house. Raja bounded ahead of him. He always went with Raki to school. Together they started climbing the steep path up the mountain.

Five miles to school. Every day except Sunday, Raki walked five miles to school; and in the evening, he walked home again. There was no school in his own small village of Koli, for the village consisted of only five families. The nearest school was in the small town of Chamoli. Raki's village lay in the valley below Chamoli, and a steep footpath was the only link between the village and the town.

In Chamoli there was a school, a small hospital, a post office, and several shops. In Koli village there were none of these. If you were sick, you stayed at home until you got well. If you were very sick, you walked or were carried to the hospital, up the five-mile path. If you wanted something, you went without it. If you wanted it very badly, you could walk to Chamoli.

Koli was known as the Five Mile Village.

Twice a week the postman came to the village. Raki usually passed him on his way to and from school.

Leaving the village and the fields below him, Raki climbed steadily up the path. By the time the sun was up, he had entered the welcome shade of a forest of oaks and rhododendrons. Raja went bounding ahead, chasing squirrels and barking at monkeys.

Emerging from the trees, Raki stopped to drink the fresh, clean water of a spring. Here he met Beenu, a boy from a neighbouring village.

Beenu had two large milk cans slung over his shoulders. Every morning he carried his milk to town, selling some to the school and some to Dr Taylor, the lady doctor at the hospital.

They hailed each other and Beenu fell into step beside Raki. They often met near the spring, walking together to Chamoli.

'There was a leopard prowling about our village last night,' said Beenu.

Raki was interested but not excited. Leopards were often seen in the hills, and occasionally one of them would take to prowling about the outskirts of a village, seizing a careless dog or a stray goat.

'Did you lose any animals?' asked Raki.

'No. It tried to get into the cowshed but the dogs set up an alarm. We drove it off.'

'It must be the same leopard that came around last winter. We lost a calf and two dogs in our village.'

'Wasn't that the one the hunters wounded?'

'It could be the same. It has a bullet in its leg. It can't move fast enough to catch the deer and wild animals.'

'We are lucky it hasn't become a man-eater. Do you remember the man-eater six years ago?'

'I was very small then,' said Raki. 'My father told me about it. Ten people were killed in the valley. What happened to it?'

'I don't know. Some say it poisoned itself when it ate the moneylender in our village.'

They linked arms and scrambled up the stony path. Raja began barking and ran ahead. Someone was coming down the path.

It was the postman.

'Any letters for us?' asked Raki and Beenu together.

They never received any letters but that did not discourage them from asking.

'You can have them all,' said the postman, 'if you will carry my bag for me.'

'We would gladly carry your bag,' said Raki, 'but we're going in the opposite direction!'

The postman, complaining of sore feet, continued on his way, and the boys continued their climb. It was eight o'clock when they reached Chamoli. Dr Taylor's out-patients were just beginning to line up at the hospital gate. Dr Taylor was fifty, white-haired but fresh in the face and full of energy. She had been in India for over twenty years, working in the remote hill regions where few doctors care to go.

She saw Raki coming down the road. She knew about him and his long walk to school.

Raki greeted her shyly. Raja barked and put his paws up on the gate.

'Yes, there's a bone for you,' said the doctor. 'You can collect it later.'

The school bell was ringing and Raki broke into a run. Raja loped along behind him.

When Raki entered the school gate, Raja sat down on the grass of the compound. He would remain there until the lunch break. He knew of various ways of amusing himself during school hours and had friends among the bazaar dogs.

2

Mr Joshi, Raki's teacher, was in a bad mood. He prided himself on his rose garden, and that morning, looking out of his bedroom window, he had been horrified to see a herd of goats in his garden. He had chased them down the road with a stick but the damage had already been done. His prize roses had all been eaten.

Mr Joshi was so upset that he had gone without his breakfast. He had also cut himself while shaving. His mood had gone from bad to worse. Several times during the day he used his ruler on the knuckles of the more mischievous boys. Raki was one of his best pupils. But even Raki got a whack from the ruler, simply for asking too many questions. That was the kind of day it was for their teacher...

'Poor Mr Joshi,' thought Raki. 'I wonder why he is so upset. Perhaps he hasn't received his pay.'

Armed with a bundle of homework, Raki came out from the school compound at four o'clock, and was immediately joined by Raja, who had already collected his bone from Dr Taylor. They did not stay long in the bazaar. There were five miles to walk, and Raki's mother did not like him coming home after dark.

Beenu had gone home long ago, and Raki had to make the return journey on his own. He had reached the little spring when he remembered the bangles he had promised to buy for his sister.

'Oh, I've forgotten them again,' he said aloud. 'Now I'll catch it! And she has probably made something special for my dinner!'

Raja, to whom these words were addressed, paid no attention but bounded off into the oak forest. Raki looked around for the monkeys but they were nowhere to be seen.

'That's strange,' he thought. 'I wonder why they have disappeared.'

Suddenly he heard a sharp cry, followed by a long yelp. He knew at once that Raja was in trouble. The sound came from the bushes down the steep hillside, where Raja had rushed a few seconds before.

In the fading light, Raki jumped off the path and ran down the slope towards the bushes. There was no dog. He whistled and called but there was no response. Then he saw something lying on the dry grass. He picked it up. It was part of Raja's collar.

Raki did not search further. He knew, without a doubt, that Raja had been seized by a leopard. No other animal could have attacked so silently and swiftly, carrying off a big dog with hardly a struggle. Raja must have been dead within seconds of being caught.

Raki knew the danger that lay in wait for him if he tried to follow the leopard. It would attack anyone who tried to interfere with its meal.

With tears starting in his eyes, he began running down the path to his village. His fingers still clutched the little bit of collar that was all that was left to him of his dog.

It is a hard life for people living in the Himalayan valleys, and the children are not very sentimental; but Raki sorrowed for his dog. He did not sleep that night but turned restlessly from side to side. After some time he felt Puja's hand in his own. The touch of her rough, familiar hand comforted him.

Next morning when he went down to the stream to bathe, he missed the presence of his dog. He did not stay long in the water. It wasn't so much fun when there was no Raja to watch him.

When Rakis mother gave him his food, she told him to be careful and to hurry home that evening. A leopard, even if it is only a lifter of sheep or dogs, is not to be taken lightly; and this particular leopard had been unusually daring in seizing the dog while it was still daylight.

There was no question of staying away from school. If Raki remained at home every time a leopard put in an appearance, he might just as well stop going to school altogether.

He set off earlier than usual and reached the spring long before Beenu. He did not wait for his friend, because he did not feel like talking about the loss of his dog. It was not the day for the postman, so Raki reached Chamoli without meeting anyone on the way. He tried to slip past the hospital gate unnoticed but Dr Taylor saw him, and the first thing she said was, 'Where's Raja? I've got something for him.'

When Dr Taylor saw the boy's face, she knew at once that something was wrong.

'What is it, Raki?' she asked. She looked quickly up and down the road. 'What happened to Raja?'

'A leopard took him,' said Raki.

'Where?'

'In the forest, while I was walking home.'

Raki turned away and began running down the road to school.

His schoolmates questioned him about Raja's absence. He had to tell them everything. There was a lot of noise and excitement in the classroom and Mr Joshi had to call for order. When he learned what had happened, he patted Raki on the head and told him that he need not attend school for the rest of the day. But Raki did not want to go home. After school, he got into a fight with one of the boys and that helped him to forget.

3

Nine-year-old Sanjay, a friend of Raki's, was the first person in Koli to be attacked by the leopard.

Sanjay's house was the last in the village and nearest the stream. Like the other houses, it was quite small, just a room above and a stable below, with steps leading up from outside the house.

One evening, not long after Raja had been taken by the leopard, Sanjay brought his father's cows home after grazing them on the hill slopes. He and his small brothers had their food at dusk, sitting on the floor of their single room, and soon afterwards settled down for the night. Sanjay curled up in his favourite spot, with his head near the door to get the fresh air. As the summer nights were quite warm, the door was usually left slightly open. Sanjay's mother piled ash on the embers of the fire, and the family was soon asleep.

No one heard the stealthy padding of the leopard approaching the door, pushing it open. Suddenly there were sounds of struggle. Sanjay's cries mingled with the snarls of the animal.

Sanjay's father leapt to his feet with a shout. The leopard had dragged the boy outside. The father rushed out on to the steps, picked up a heavy grinding-stone and struck at the animal. Everyone in the house was shouting. A number of people from the neighbouring houses came rushing to their assistance. As soon as the leopard saw them, it let the boy go and bounded away.

Sanjay lay unconscious on the steps.

But he was alive.

His father smeared ash on the boy's head to stop the bleeding, while his mother tore strips off her homespun dress to make a bandage. Long before it was dawn, Sanjay's father, with the boy on his back, had set off for the Chamoli hospital. Three or four men accompanied them, armed with sticks and axes.

They roused Dr Taylor, and the boy's father stammered out an account of what had happened. The doctor cleaned and dressed the wound and gave Sanjay a shot of penicillin to prevent infection.

'You brought him in good time,' she said. 'He'll be all right. The wounds will heal. We'll keep him here in the hospital until he recovers.'

After this attack, the leopard went away for some time. But the people of Koli could not be sure of its whereabouts. They kept to their houses after dark, and shut all their doors. Raki had to stop going to school, as there was no one to accompany him and it was dangerous to go alone. This worried him, because his exams were only a few weeks off and he would be missing important classwork. When he wasn't in the fields, helping with the sowing of rice and maize, he sat in the shade of a cherry tree, going through his well-thumbed schoolbooks.

Sanjay was recovering quickly and was able to come home

after a week. With his little face covered by a huge bandage, he looked rather helpless; but he was getting better and the wound was healing.

Two weeks passed, and no one had seen the leopard. People were beginning to hope that it might have moved on, over the mountain or further down the valley.

'I think I can start going to school again,' said Raki. 'The leopard has gone away.'

'Don't be so sure,' said Puja. 'There's a full moon these days. It might be waiting for the dark nights.'

'Yes, wait a few days,' said his mother. 'It is better to wait. Perhaps you could go the day after tomorrow, when Sanjay goes to the hospital with his father for a check-up. Then you will have company.'

So, two days later, Raki went up to Chamoli with Sanjay and his father. Sanjay's wound had almost healed. Dr Taylor said he could come again after a week.

Raki went to his school and was given a warm welcome by his friends and by Mr Joshi.

'You must work hard and catch up with the class,' said Mr Joshi. 'If you like, I can give you some extra time after class.'

'Thank you, sir, but it will make me late,' said Raki. 'My mother will worry if I do not get home before dark.'

'Well, you had better not take any risks. Work hard, and you'll soon catch up with your lessons.'

Sanjay and his father were waiting for him outside the school. Together they took the path down to Koli, passing the postman on his way. The postman said that he had heard that the leopard had crossed into another valley and that there was nothing to fear.

Nothing happened on the way home. The monkeys were

back in their favourite part of the forest. Raki got back just as the kerosene lamp was being lit by his mother. Puja met him at the door with a winning smile.

'Did you get the bangles?' she asked.

But Raki had forgotten again.

4

There had been a thunderstorm, and the sharp summer shower gave the villagers hope that the monsoon would arrive on time.

Raki, on his way home from school, was caught in the rain. He knew the shower would not last very long, so he took shelter in a small cave.

When the rain stopped, he left the cave and continued on his way. He wasn't in a hurry. The rain had made everything smell fresh and good. A flock of parrots swept across the hill, and the monkeys leapt from tree to tree.

He was almost out of the forest when he heard a faint bleating. A little goat was stumbling up the path towards him. The kid must have strayed from a herd. It came to Raki with a little hop, skip and a jump, and rubbed against his legs.

'I wonder who you belong to,' mused Raki, stroking the kid. 'I'd better keep you with me, or you'll get lost.'

Darkness was coming on and Raki walked a little faster, the kid following close behind him.

He had not gone far when he heard a strange sound. It was like a saw cutting through wood—the long harsh breathing of a leopard on the prowl.

The sound came from Raki's right, from a distance of fifty to sixty yards. Raki hesitated on the path, wondering what he should do. Then he picked the kid up in his arms, and began running.

He heard the leopard again, much closer now. He looked up and down the hillside. The forest was some way behind and only a few trees covered the steep slopes. Raki made for a spruce.

The branches of the Himalayan spruce are very brittle and snap easily beneath a heavy weight. They were strong enough to support Raki's light body. He hoped they would not support the weight of a leopard.

Holding the kid with one arm, Raki gripped a low branch and swung himself up into the tree. He was a good climber. He climbed halfway up the tree, till he was about twelve feet off the ground. He couldn't go any higher without risking a fall.

He had barely settled himself in the crook of a branch when the leopard ran into the clearing. This was no stealthy approach or careful stalking of its prey. It was a man-eater all right. A shiver ran down Raki's spine.

The leopard stood in the clearing, its head thrust slightly forward. It had the appearance of gazing intently and rather short-sightedly at some invisible object in the clearing. But there is nothing short-sighted about a leopard's vision: both sight and hearing are acute.

Raki remained motionless in the tree but the kid began to bleat. The leopard looked up. A deep rasping sound came from its throat. It was trying to frighten the boy into falling from the tree. Many a monkey has fallen to its doom in this way.

The leopard did not try to leap into the tree. Perhaps it knew that this was not the kind of tree that it could climb easily. Instead it walked a semi-circle around the tree, keeping its head turned towards Raki.

Raki did not flinch. He remembered an expression his father sometimes used—'always look a tiger in the eye'—and he stared down at the hard blunt shape of the leopard's head.

Suddenly the leopard disappeared into some bushes.

Although Raki knew that this was just another trick on the part of the leopard, he could not help giving a sigh of relief. And how he longed to be at home, secure behind a heavy door, the lamp burning, and his mother and Puja at his side!

He heard a crackling sound in the trees, and stiffened. He was sure the man-eater was crouching there, watching him. Peering into the darkness, he thought he could make out two glowing eyes staring at him from the bushes. Then he realized that his imagination was playing tricks. The light came from a pair of fireflies, moving slowly through the trees.

The kid was restless and Raki was having difficulty in preventing it from leaping out of his arms.

The cunning man-eater tried to catch Raki off his guard. With a low growl, it rushed back into the clearing. Then it stopped, staring up at Raki in surprise.

The leopard was getting impatient. Snarling, it put its forefeet up against the tree trunk, and began scratching at the bark. The tree shook at each thud of the animal's paws.

It was then that Raki began shouting for help.

◆

The moon had not yet risen. Down in Koli, Raki's mother and sister stood in their lighted doorway, gazing anxiously up the path. Every now and then Puja would go inside to check the time.

Sanjay's father appeared in a field below. He held a lamp.

'Isn't your boy home yet?' he asked.

'No, we are very worried. He should have been home an hour ago. Do you think that leopard will be about tonight?'

'It's a dark night. The leopard could be about. I'll fetch

some of the other men and we will go up the mountain for your boy. There may have been a landslide due to the rain. Perhaps the path has been washed away. Don't worry, we'll bring him home safely.'

'Thank you. But arm yourselves well.'

'I am coming too,' said Puja.

'No, you must not go,' said her mother. 'It's bad enough that Raki may be in danger. You stay at home with me.'

'I shall be safe with the menfolk,' said Puja. 'I'm going, mother!' And she jumped down the embankment into the field and followed Sanjay's father down the village lane.

Muttering a prayer, Raki's mother watched them as they disappeared into the darkness. Several lamps appeared and could be seen bobbing up the hill as a small group of people moved silently up the mountain path. Puja walked in the middle of the group, holding a lamp. The men carried staves and axes. As soon as the village was left behind, the men began to shout—both to frighten off the leopard if it was about, and to give themselves courage.

Raki's calls were carried on the wind, and Puja and the men heard him while they were still half a mile away. Their own shouts increased in volume. Hearing them, Raki felt strength return to his trembling limbs. Growing in confidence, he began shouting insults at the snarling leopard. Then he threw twigs and small branches at the furious animal.

As the search party drew near, they heard the leopard's snarls and hurried forward. Puja began to run.

'Don't rush ahead, girl,' said Sanjay's father. 'Stay between us.'

The leopard, now aware of the approaching humans, stood still in the middle of the clearing, its head thrust forward. There seemed to be too many men for one leopard.

When it saw the light of the lamps dancing between the trees, the animal turned, snarling hate and defiance, and without another look at the boy in the tree, disappeared into the shadows.

5

The man-eater did not lose much time in finding another victim.

One morning Beenu came running down the path, babbling excitedly about the postman.

Beenu had been grazing his cattle on the hillside when he stumbled across the postman's mailbag lying on the ground. But of the postman there was no sign. He had been dragged away through the bushes.

A week after the postman's disappearance, an old woman who was out gathering dry sticks for firewood was taken by the leopard.

It seemed that there was little that anyone could do about the man-eater. The villagers had no guns, and it would take days, even weeks, for experienced hunters to reach the valley.

Raki was unhappy because he could not go to school. Many boys would be only too happy to miss school; but for a boy living in a remote mountain village, getting through school is the only way of seeing the world some day. And Raki liked going to school, even though it was five miles from home.

'Cheer up, brother,' said Puja, bringing him a glass of hot sweet tea. 'The leopard may go elsewhere once the rains break.'

'Even the monsoon is late this year,' said Raki. 'It's so hot and dry. Can't we open the door?'

'And have the leopard walk in?' asked their mother. 'It isn't safe to have the window open, let alone the door.' She went to the tiny window and bolted it firmly. But the skylight remained open. Through it Raki was just able to see the crescent moon.

Complaining of the heat, Raki threw off most of his clothes and stretched himself out on the earthen floor.

'We will be rid of the beast before long,' said his mother. 'I know it in my heart. Our prayers will be heard, and you shall go to school and pass your exams.'

In the middle of the night, Raki woke up. He could hear his sister's easy breathing and the ticking of the clock. Far away, an owl hooted. He wondered what could have woken him.

And then he heard something scratching at the door.

It was like a cat scratching, only louder. The door creaked a little under the impact of a heavy paw.

'It's the leopard,' he said under his breath, sitting up on the floor.

Suddenly Raki was angry, angrier than he had ever been before, and all his fear was gone.

'Just who does he think he is, coming right up to my door?' he said aloud.

Across the room, resting against the wall, was his father's old spear-pole—a long bamboo stick with a sharp knife tied to one end, which Raki sometimes used for spearing fish. He moved toward it quietly, so as not to wake his mother and sister. Grasping the home-made spear, he scrambled on to a small cupboard and drew level with the skylight. He could just get his head and shoulders through the narrow opening.

'What are you doing up there?' whispered Puja, who had woken up.

'Be quiet,' said Raki. 'Don't wake mother.'

But their mother was already awake. 'Come down from there, Raki. I can hear a noise outside.'

'It's nothing,' said Raki, looking down at the leopard still trying to get its paw under the door. He had managed to get the spear through the skylight, and was pointing it at the leopard's head.

'I'll teach you a lesson,' said Raki, and he flung the spear as hard as he could.

Just at that moment the leopard turned, and the spear missed the head. Instead it landed just above the tail. The leopard let out a roar of pain and rage, and leapt down the steps and into the bushes, not pausing to see what had struck it.

Three days passed and nobody heard or saw the man-eater. Raki had retrieved his spear from the bottom of the steps where it had fallen.

'I knew it was a coward,' he said. 'Just like any bully, brave enough until he gets hurt! I think I'll go to school tomorrow.'

'Wait a few more days,' said Puja.

'No more waiting,' said Raki. 'I'll be waiting all my life if I let that leopard bother me. It's school tomorrow, Puja! And this time I won't forget your bangles.'

That evening Puja was hoeing the last field above the house. Raki, at the other end of the same field, was chopping wood. The slanting sun glinted in patches on the stream below.

Pausing for a moment to wipe the sweat from his brow, Raki glanced up at the hillside. His eye fell on a round rock on the brow of the hill which seemed unfamiliar to him. Just as he was about to look away, the rock began to grow and then alter its shape. Watching in fascination, Raki was at last able to make out the head and forequarters of some animal. It looked very big from the angle at which he saw it, and for a moment he thought it was a tiger.

But Raki knew instinctively that it was the man-eating leopard.

Slowly the cunning beast got to its feet and began to walk around the side of the great rock. For a second it disappeared and Raki wondered if it had gone away. Then it reappeared, moving swiftly across the face of the rock until it was in a direct line with the corner of the field where Puja was working.

Raki realised that the leopard was stalking his sister.

He ran forward, shouting, 'Run, Puja, run!'

Puja turned to see what Raki was shouting about. She saw him gesture at the hill behind her, and looked up just in time to see the leopard crouching for its spring.

Puja leapt down the banking of the field and tumbled into an irrigation ditch.

The springing leopard tried to change direction, lost its foothold on the slippery banking, and slithered into the ditch a few feet away from Puja. At the same time Raki came dashing down the slope, swinging his axe.

Others in the fields had seen what was happening, and three men came running across the field with axes. They thrust Raki aside and made a half-circle around the snarling man-eater. Puja wriggled along the ditch on her stomach.

The leopard turned at bay and plunged at the men, but received several blows before it broke through the cordon and crashed into the bushes. The men followed it, shouting to each other to be careful. Raki was close behind them.

The wounded leopard had made for the bed of the stream, and here they were able to follow it quite easily, along the rocks which were spotted with blood. After some time they found the leopard lying very still on its side at the edge of the water.

'It is dead,' said Raki. 'It will not trouble us again.'

As the sun set, a big fire was lit in the middle of the village, and everyone gathered round it, singing and laughing. Sanjay's father killed a fat goat, and there was a feast for all the Village.

6

Raki was on his way home. He had just done his first exam paper, without much difficulty. Mr Joshi and the entire class were happy that he had been able to take his exams. He was a heroto them for his part in ridding the valley of the man-eater.

He walked past the hospital, whistling cheerfully. Dr Taylor waved to him from the verandah steps.

'How is Sanjay now?' she asked.

'He is well,' said Raki.

'And your mother and sister?'

'They are well.'

He started down the path to the village. Dark clouds had gathered and there was a rumble of thunder.

'Wait for me!' shouted Beenu, his milk cans clanging, as he ran after Raki.

'We must hurry,' said Raki. 'It's going to rain heavily.'

'I feel like getting wet,' said Beenu. 'The monsoon has arrived, I'm sure.'

Big drops were falling when they reached the parting of the paths and waved goodbye to each other.

Raki entered the forest alone and at that moment the rain came down in heavy sheets. The trees shook in the Wind. The monkeys chattered with excitement.

Raki was drenched to the skin. But just as the village of Koli came into view, the rain stopped suddenly. The sun appeared through a rift in the clouds. The leaves and the grass gave out a fresh sweet smell.

Raki could see his mother and sister in their field, transplanting the rice seedlings. In other fields, men were driving their yoked oxen through the thin mud, while small children hung on to the animals' tails, standing on the plain wooden harrows, and with wild shouts sending the animals at a gallop along the narrow terraces.

Raki ran down the path, his feet falling softly on the wet earth. Puja saw him coming and waved to him. She met him at the edge of the field.

'How did you find your exam paper today?' she asked.

'Oh, it was easy.' Raki slipped his hand into hers and together they walked across the field.

Puja felt something smooth and round against her fingers and looked down to see a pair of bangles in her hand.

'I remembered,' said Raki triumphantly.

Puja looked at the bangles and burst out: 'But these are blue, brother, and I wanted red and gold bangles!' And then, when she saw him looking crestfallen, she added: 'But they are very pretty, and you *did* remember... Come, I have made something special for you today.'